A Cup of
CHRISTMAS
CHEER

VOLUME TWO

A Cup of

CHRISTMAS CHEER

TALES of JOY and WONDER
for the HOLIDAYS

Guideposts

New York

A Cup of Christmas Cheer is a trademark of Guideposts.

Published by Guideposts
110 William Street
New York, NY 10038
Guideposts.org

Acknowledgments

Every attempt has been made to credit the sources of copyrighted material used in this book. If any such acknowledgment has been inadvertently omitted or miscredited, receipt of such information would be appreciated.

Cover and interior design by Müllerhaus
Illustrated by Greg Copeland, represented by Deborah Wolfe LTD
Typeset by Aptara, Inc.

Printed and bound in the United States of America
10 9 8 7 6 5 4 3 2

Contents

MEAT LOAF AND OTHER MINOR MIRACLES

Liz Johnson

Caitlyn Peters chuckled when her fiancé, Ian, said that his dad always requested meat loaf and brown gravy for Christmas Eve dinner. Her laughter mingled with the gentle hum of the lunch crowd at their favorite East Nashville bistro. "That's nice."

"Mom and Dad can't wait to meet you next week." His smile grew wide as his gaze dropped to her hand, which rested lightly on the red-and-white-checked tablecloth beside her bag of leftovers.

Rubbing her thumb along the underside of her left ring finger, she followed the curve of cool platinum. The weight of the diamond on top of the simple band was still unusual, but that didn't mean she had any intention of taking it off. Ever.

She'd waited too long to meet such an amazing man. Thirty-three years, to be exact. "I'm looking forward to meeting them too." A tiny butterfly in her stomach escaped, bouncing along an uncertain path that belied the truth of her statement. Of course she was excited. And nervous. And maybe a little bit petrified. They were everything she was not—Southern royalty.

Well, Ian had assured her his parents weren't exactly royalty, but his grandfather had been one of Georgia's most popular governors. As a hometown champion of The Masters Golf Tournament, Ian's dad had literally had a parade in his honor. And as far as Caitlyn could deduce, Ian's mom sounded like a former Miss America. Her talent portion had doubtless featured her culinary flair.

Of course, they must be very nice people. After all, they'd raised an amazingly kind and compassionate son. But would they approve of his Yankee-transplant fiancée, who was more at home shoveling snow than sipping sweet tea?

Ian glanced at his watch. "I've got to get back to work. But I'll see you tomorrow?" She stood as well, slipping on her jacket and pulling her scarf close around her throat. With her doggie bag in one hand, she tucked the other into the warm embrace of his.

"Thanks for meeting me for lunch, honey. And for agreeing to host Christmas Eve with my parents."

"Any time." Peppermint tea and marshmallowed hot cocoa with her soon-to-be in-laws as the clock rolled closer to Christmas morning could be the perfect first impression. She couldn't mess that up.

She leaned in for his kiss, as warm as a cup of cocoa on this blustery day.

Giving her arm one final squeeze, he said. "I'm sure Dad is going to love your meat loaf."

"My what?" But her whispered words were met only by his wave as he hurried back to his office.

Blinking several times, she finally closed her gaping mouth and swallowed the disbelief that bubbled up, burning as it rose to her throat. The chills running down her arms and legs had little to do with the December weather and nearly everything to do with the mess she'd just landed in.

When had she agreed to cook them dinner?

If Ian hadn't noticed in their six months together that she didn't cook, he hadn't been paying attention.

But he had been. She'd caught him watching her with eyes full of careful intent, always searching her out when he entered a room. His gaze followed her stride as she walked, like a gentle caress on the nape of her neck. She knew he'd been watching her because she'd been watching him the same way since they met.

So what on earth had possessed him to think she could cook his dad's favorite meat loaf and fixin's?

She let out a quick breath of air, sending her bangs skyward, and clutched the only thing she'd ever been any good at making—leftovers—as she scurried past the young man at the corner strumming on his guitar and singing about dreaming of snow for Christmas.

Dreaming wouldn't be enough to help her. Either she'd get a Christmas miracle in the form of culinary skills, or she'd have to disappoint the family she most wanted to impress.

It was time to start praying for that miracle.

* * *

Whoever said that practice could make perfect conveniently forgot to specify the amount of practice required. Caitlyn had rehearsed her speech at least fifteen times, positive it would convince him to rescue her from certain disaster. But when Ian called with details straight from his mother's recipe cards, her practiced words failed her.

Before she knew it, she happily agreed—again—to make the meal of his childhood. The meal he'd grown up drooling over. The meal he couldn't wait for her to make every Christmas Eve for the rest of their lives.

"I love you," he said before hanging up. And she knew it to be true. He did love her. And she, him. It wasn't his fault she'd failed to honestly express her...culinary distress.

Or that her fear of failing to prepare an edible meal had turned all anticipation for meeting his parents into a lump the size of China in her stomach.

Leaning her forearms against the white and black-tiled kitchen counter, she reviewed the list of dishes she'd jotted on her magnetic shopping list right below the standards: apples, yogurt, and microwave popcorn. The menu started with meat loaf with brown gravy and worked its way through collard greens, mac and cheese, black-eyed peas, bread pudding, and, of course, pecan pie.

She blinked. This was enough food to feed the entire line at the rescue mission. How could four people possibly even taste every item on the menu?

Rubbing her hands together, she stared at the row of brightly colored cookbooks atop the white refrigerator. Dust flew into the air as she pulled down the one with the red-and-white cover.

Flipping to the Southern side dish section of her cookbook, she held her pen poised to write down all the tips for conquering this meal.

She'd give them just what they wanted. She'd prove she was worthy.

She'd learn how to cook.

* * *

Caitlyn ran a finger along the wall of spices at the grocery store. All the names ran together, a jumble of indeterminate descriptions. Garlic salt. Garlic powder. Whole garlic cloves. All she'd written on her shopping list was *garlic*.

Glancing at the industrial-inspired ceiling, she sent up a prayer for a divine intervention. The only response was the tinny Christmas carols pumped through the speakers, wishing joy to the world and peace on earth.

But all she really wanted for Christmas was an edible meat loaf.

And whatever kind of garlic it required.

"You look lost."

Caitlyn turned to the woman pushing the neighboring grocery cart. "Is it that obvious?"

The woman chuckled, fine wrinkles forming at the corners of her pale-blue eyes. "Only a bit." A Southern accent draped each word like fresh honey on warm biscuits. "What are you looking for?"

"Garlic?"

The Southern belle lifted two perfectly arched eyebrows toward her halo of blonde curls. "You don't sound at all sure about that."

"I have no idea what I need." Laughing, Caitlyn pressed a hand to her cheek. "I just wrote down garlic, but then I got here. There are all these choices, and I tried to look up a recipe on my phone, but my battery is dead. And it would probably be the wrong recipe anyway. And I don't really have any idea what I'm doing."

The brows slowly rose until the surprise on the beautiful face could not be mistaken.

"And now I've scared you. I'm sorry."

Why did her mouth insist on doing its own thing? First, it refused to tell Ian the words she'd clearly rehearsed. Now she was rambling on to a perfectly nice stranger, who—if that glint in her eye was any indication—was about half a second away from bolting toward the trombone-playing bell ringer at the front door.

"Not at all." Her smile transformed her face from merely pretty to nearly breathtaking. As she turned, the overhead lights caught on a shimmering brooch—an angel outlined in rubies and diamonds—pinned at her collar. Though probably nearing sixty, the years had done nothing to dim the joy and delight that radiated across her features. "You're not the first young lady to be lost in the spice section, and you certainly won't be the last. Now, what exactly are you looking for?"

Turning back to the wall of confusion, Caitlyn pulled several bottles from the rack. "What would I use for meat loaf?"

The woman reached for one of the jars, then snatched her hand back, resting it against her throat. "Meat loaf? Oh, you'll need fresh garlic for that."

"Fresh?"

"I'll show you." The kind stranger set off, gliding toward the edge of the store, with Caitlyn in pursuit.

Her new friend finally stopped in front of a bin divided in sections for white onions, red onions, unidentified little green sprouts, and lumpy white bulbs. With a practiced grip, her friend squeezed a papery white globe, and waved it beneath her nose. "What do you think?"

Caitlyn blinked, surprised to be asked her opinion. She fumbled it before holding it near her face and inhaling. Odd. The bland smell and flaky white covering didn't even hint at the spicy aroma of her favorite restaurant's garlic chicken. "Good?"

"Does it feel mushy or too dry?"

She pinched it. "No?"

Another bulb hid most of her new friend's radiant smile, and she pointed at a roll of plastic. "Go ahead and put it in a bag then."

They repeated the first steps until garlic covered the bottom of the sack.

"Thank you for your help."

"A pleasure, my dear." With a wink, the gracious woman pushed her cart away.

Returning the grin, Caitlyn set the bag into her basket and turned back to her list, checking off the first item. Only three dozen more foreign items to find.

She wandered the aisles as though she'd never shopped in a grocery store. Except, of course, she had. She'd just never needed such specific ingredients. After the help of her very own garlic angel, however, it wasn't quite so intimidating. Maybe the peppermint scent wafting from a plate loaded with samples in the bakery section cheered her. Or perhaps the child in the cereal aisle dashing right along with a sleigh ride carol. Music and laughter mingled, and for just a moment she forgot why she'd been so nervous.

Until she reached the back wall, covered with cases of meat. Frozen. Fresh. Seafood. Chicken. Beef. From ground rounds to the finest filets, boneless, skinless, smell-less—she was clueless.

How could she ever select the proper meat for the traditional Christmas Eve meat loaf? At least she didn't have to contend with every other customer digging through the remnants in the turkey bin.

"I had that first!" A nearby woman yelled, pulling on the mesh handle of an Olympic-sized turkey.

The man holding on to the body of the bird refused give in. "My wife'll kill me if I don't come home with the biggest one they've got." The fear in his eyes suggested that his wife would make good on her threat.

Caitlyn cringed. At least she wasn't fighting for a turkey or scrabbling through the depleted ham selection. She needed beef. Just some beef. But she couldn't get to the frozen display without shoving her cart through a tug-of-war.

There had to be another way.

"Help you, ma'am?" A jolly man wearing a white jacket and hair net leaned forward from the other side of a glass case.

"Yes. I mean, I hope so." Dipping and crouching, Caitlyn eyed every option and little yellow price tag. More expensive meant better quality, right? Leaner cuts were healthier. But was she supposed to buy a cut and grind it herself? How?

Jerry—his name embroidered on the jacket—rested both arms on top of the glass, folding his hands below his pleasant jowls. "Better to have a good steak than fight over a turkey, I always say." Humor laced his words, and Caitlyn smiled in kind. "Now, what can I do for you?"

"Umm..." She crossed her arms and fought back the tears that stung the corner of her eyes.

She was a grown woman, a successful architect, and a volunteer at the public library. If she could design a building, she could pick out a slab of beef. Especially with professional help.

"I have to make meat loaf, but not just any meat loaf. It has to be perfect. What do you recommend?"

Lifting a shoulder, he asked, "What do you like?"

Her stomach fell to her toes, and her words leaked out on a sigh, as lost as she felt. "I have no idea."

Before Jerry could offer sage butcher wisdom, something barreled into her cart, shoving the handle into her ribs. She jumped and covered the sharp pain in her side, only to smack her elbow into someone else.

"I'm so sorry," she said before recognizing the victim of her flying elbow as her garlic angel.

"No harm done." The blonde halo wasn't even tilted as she patted Caitlyn's arm. "Were you hurt?"

"No. Just surprised."

"Good." The older woman glanced over her shoulder toward the turkey-inspired mayhem. "I hope you're staying out of that brawl."

Caitlyn nodded, wishing that her selection was as easy as plastic-wrapped poultry, even if it did come with a few battle wounds.

"So just the meat loaf for Christmas then?"

"I guess."

The woman let out a chirp of laughter that lit her face. "You don't sound very sure of that. Lucky for you, I'm something of a meat loaf expert."

"You are?" Hope bubbled up in her chest. Maybe. Maybe her meal wouldn't be a flop. Maybe she could impress Ian's parents. Maybe she could show his mother she was worthy of the family?

"My friends call me Dottie." She held out her hand.

"I'm Caitlyn Peters."

"Well, Caitlyn Peters. I'm so pleased to know you."

She squinted into the pretty face, a strange sensation sweeping from her head to her feet, like a gentle breeze dancing across her skin. "I'm sorry, but do we...have we met before?" Dottie glanced toward the produce section, and Caitlyn laughed, waving a hand toward it. "I mean before the garlic incident."

"I don't think so. I'd remember someone with your smile."

And then, of course, Caitlyn could do nothing but smile in response.

"Now." Dottie's eyebrows pulled together, her face transforming into work mode. "Meat loaf, you say?"

"That's right. With brown gravy."

Something akin to bewilderment slipped across the graceful features, but she said only, "You'll need high-quality ground beef, not too lean or it will end up dry. How many people will you be serving?"

"Four."

Again, a wisp of mystification crossed Dottie's face. "Then a pound and a half should be plenty for dinner and leftovers."

"I love leftovers." Caitlyn slapped a hand over her mouth. Had she really just announced her penchant for reheated meals to a proper Southern belle?

Dottie winked. "Me too." Then she pointed at the middle of the display window and looked Jerry right in the eye. "We'll have a pound and a half of the eighty-five percent ground beef."

As the butcher measured and wrapped up the key to the perfect Christmas Eve meal, Caitlyn said, "How did you do that?"

One finely arched brow rose. "I just ordered some meat. Jerry is doing all the hard work."

"But you just decided. You were so confident. You just *knew* what to get. How do you know it will turn out?"

"Oh, sweetie." She took the paper-wrapped package from Jerry and handed it to Caitlyn. "The unknown is half the joy of cooking." As an afterthought, she added, "And life. Don't you think?"

Well, she'd never really thought of it before, and Caitlyn certainly hadn't thought of making this meal in any context of fun. So she shrugged and gave a half smile.

With hands on her hips, Dottie shook her head. "You don't look very energetic. Your food will only taste as vibrant as you feel while you're cooking. If you're not excited about cooking it, why should your guests be excited about eating it?"

She couldn't help a quick glance at Dottie's cart, which held a stack of red boxes, each a single serving of chicken-fried steak and green beans or some other equally well-preserved meat-and-vegetable combination. Just the kind of meal that Ian and his bachelor friends had on hand for those nights at home in front of the television. How did a woman stocking up on premade meals know so much about the culinary arts?

"Would you like some help finishing up your list?"

How could a stranger be so kind? Was it the spirit of the season, or was she just a genuinely kind soul?

Regardless, Caitlyn wasn't going to turn down the offer. "Oh yes."

Dottie held out her hand. "Let's see your list again." As she scanned the as-yet unmarked items, her eyes widened and her smile grew. When Dottie's head tilted back up, her teeth flashed, a new sparkle in her eyes. "Well, this is enough food for an army. I suppose we should get to work." A wave of the hand and they were off. "Follow me."

There wasn't an area of the store that Dottie didn't know, though she didn't seem all that familiar with the lay-out, often looking down an aisle before shaking her head and moving on. When they arrived to the right location, she chattered on about why this potato had the best flavor and that cornstarch made lumpy gravy. The whole time her hands fluttered along the shelves, dropping the necessities into the cart.

For forty-five blissful minutes Caitlyn forgot what was on the line. She forgot that a failed meal could spell another failed relationship.

But as they pulled Caitlyn's full cart—and Dottie's nearly empty one—toward the checkout lanes, fear rushed back at Dottie's friendly benediction.

"I'm sure you'll have a great time making the meal for your family."

Dottie's tone was kind, but the truth smacked Caitlyn like she'd run into a wall. Sure, she had all of the ingredients, but she had no practical experience in preparing the meal. She lurched to a halt, and Dottie's cart slammed into her.

"Oh my word!" Dottie rushed to her side. "Are you all right?"

"Yes." The back of her throat burned, and she pressed flat fingers to her forehead, smoothing out the tension wrinkles there. "I'm fine. I just…"

Like a mother hen leading her chick to safety, Dottie shimmied them to the side of the aisle until the flow of traffic resumed. With both hands on Caitlyn's shoulders, she asked, "What's the matter?"

Caitlyn bit into the corner of her bottom lip, not quite able to meet the other woman's gaze. "You've been so kind, and now I have everything I need except the experience required to pull off the perfect Christmas Eve dinner."

Resting slender fingers over her lips, Dottie narrowed her eyes. "And why does it have to be perfect?"

Even to a stranger, she couldn't form the words, couldn't confess her fear of embarrassing Ian. Her fear of rejection by another boyfriend's mother. So instead she offered a half excuse. "It's Christmas. And I'm meeting my future in-laws for the first time… But what if—"

Dipping at the knees, Dottie forced her to make eye contact. "What if what?"

"What if my meat loaf is a flop and the gravy is lumpy?"

Dottie's laughter rang out and she rubbed Caitlyn's shoulder with a gentle touch. "Well, then you'll be like every other young woman serving her first big meal."

But those other young women weren't vying for a spot in a family like Ian's. They weren't trying to impress a former Miss America or win the heart of man who loved his meat loaf. How could she possibly do this on her own?

"Would it make you feel better if I lend you a hand?"

"Yes!" The word escaped before she could truly consider what Dottie was offering, and as the realization sank in, Caitlyn sighed. "But I'm cooking on Christmas Eve. I couldn't ask you to help me when you should be with your family. That's not fair."

Dottie tilted her head back and closed her eyes. "I suppose that's true. But there's really nowhere else I'd rather be."

"Really?"

"Truly."

Caitlyn leaned against her cart and heaved a deep sigh. Oh, what a relief.

Perhaps Dottie was the answer to her prayer, her divine intervention, her Christmas miracle. And if help with a meat loaf didn't qualify as a full-scale miracle, then at least she was evidence of a minor miracle. Because with a little help, Caitlyn might just pass muster. And maybe more.

* * *

Caitlyn swayed to the instrumental Christmas carols that filled the house, crushing a garlic clove under her knife just like the cookbook had described. She wrinkled her nose against the pungent smell as juice trickled dangerously close to the edge of the cutting board. She brushed the stream back to safety with her thumb just as her phone rang. Snatching it up with her spare hand, she took a quick breath before opening her mouth to answer.

Bitter and all-consuming, the odor assaulted her. Eyes leaking, nose running, throat burning. Coughs wracked her body until she doubled over, dropping the phone onto the floor.

"Caitlyn? Are you all right?" Though disembodied and distant coming from the floor, she'd recognize Ian's voice anywhere.

"Fi-ine." A tickle in her throat sent her into another coughing fit, and she lunged to the sink to scoop water into her mouth from the faucet. Anything to wash away the smell so strong she could taste it. After a few gulps, the burning subsided and she scooped up her phone. Ian was still calling out to her. "I'm here. I'm all right. Sorry about that."

His sigh of relief carried long and heavy through the phone. "I was about the call the police."

"I'm good. Just choked on the smell of garlic."

"Are you sure?"

As she filled a glass with water and poured it down her throat, she gurgled some sort of affirmative.

"All right. I was just calling to check in. Are we still on for dinner tonight at seven?"

A quick glance at the clock confirmed her suspicion. It was nearly noon. Dottie should be there soon. If she hadn't changed her mind.

"Absolutely. I'll see you at seven. Did your parents make it to town?" Could he hear in her tone a little bit of hope that they'd been delayed?

"They arrived right on time. We're going to finish up shopping this afternoon, and then we'll be at your place."

She swallowed. "Sounds great." At least she had managed to infuse some semblance of joy into her tone.

"Listen, Cait." He cleared his throat. "Thank you. I know this isn't really your thing and that you just agreed to take on

Christmas Eve dinner for me, and I want you to know how much I appreciate it. I can't wait to be married to you."

The lump in her throat was almost too big to speak around, but she managed a quick, "Me too," before hanging up.

He was something else, and she wasn't going to lose him just because she couldn't cook. Leaning against the edge of the sink, her elbows locked, she stared through the window to the barren branches of the tree in her yard. Unlike her Christmases as a child in Pennsylvania, snow hadn't yet blanketed her lawn. In her younger years she and her father spent Christmas Eve building snowmen and then drinking her late mom's hot chocolate in front of a fire. Then as the sun began to set, they bundled up and traipsed through the snow so they could join the community church choir singing carols of Christmas cheer.

But there wasn't time to wish for snow this year. Her Christmas miracle would be smothered in brown gravy, not frosted in white.

First things first, she had to get rid of the garlic smell. Holding outstretched fingers close to her nose, she took a tentative whiff. Blinking back a rush of tears, she shoved her hand under steaming water, scrubbing kitchen soap into every crevice with her fingernails.

After three minutes, she ventured another breath through her nose.

Now she smelled like garlic lemonade. Perfect. Just perfect.

The doorbell chimed, and she hurried through the dining room and into the open living room to turn the deadbolt on the front door. When she opened it, Dottie stood on the porch, wrapped in a smart peacoat cinched at the narrow waist with a wide belt.

"You came." Caitlyn couldn't help but pull Dottie into a hug. Then she quickly jumped back, holding her hands at shoulder-height. "I'm sorry. But I'm so glad to see you."

Stepping inside, Dottie shrugged out of her coat. "Where else would I be?" Her smile grew as she laid her jacket on the arm of the couch. Running her hands over wind-swept hair, she looked toward the kitchen. "It smells like you started without me."

A lump settled into the bottom of Caitlyn's stomach. "That's me, I'm afraid. I thought I'd get the garlic chopped and now my hands smell like I harvest garlic for a living."

Dottie drifted toward the kitchen, her laughter ringing in her wake. "Oh dear. Well, that won't make a very good impression on your guests, will it?"

"Not even a little bit. But I tried to scrub it off, and it's still there."

"Maybe you could wear gloves?"

Was she serious? "To dinner?"

Dottie arched an eyebrow like she'd heard stranger ideas. Then she reached across the narrow kitchen and grabbed at the blueberry oven mitt, holding it up under her nose. Her eyes danced with mirth. "Or you could just forget to take your mitts off."

The two laughed until their sides hurt and Dottie wiped at tear-filled eyes. Caitlyn didn't dare put her hands that close to her face.

Finally Dottie pointed to the faucet. "Try rubbing your hands against the stainless steel."

"What's that supposed to do?" She shot her garlic angel a dubious look but did as instructed. Bringing her fingers back up to her nose, she flinched before taking a good breath. A lemon-scented breath.

"How did you do that?"

"I have a few tricks up my sleeve, my dear." She waved a hand. "Now, I need an apron." Caitlyn pulled one from the back of the pantry door, and Dottie tied it around her waist, covering her navy slacks and matching blue striped top. When she was settled, she put her hands on her hips. "Shall we start with the pecan pie?"

So they did. Dottie stepped back, offering suggestions as Caitlyn mixed the ingredients for the crust before slipping it into the oven. While that baked, Caitlyn brought butter, brown sugar, and corn syrup to a boil on the stove. Yet again Dottie stood close by and coached, her tips quick and easy.

When the pie crust was cooked and the filling almost complete, there was only one thing left to do. She had to add an egg. Fishing one from the fresh pack Dottie had handed her at the store just two days before, Caitlyn held it out. "Do you want to break it?"

"Go ahead."

Her hands tingled with uncertainty. "I'm not sure—I don't know that I know how."

Dottie began to laugh and then stopped immediately. "You don't know how to crack an egg?"

Shrugging, Caitlyn shook her head. "I broke one or two too many as a little girl."

"Haven't you ever made scrambled eggs or brownies?" Her pitch rose with each word, disbelief shining on her face.

Caitlyn dropped her gaze to her hand. Is this how her soon-to-be mother-in-law would react? "I guess not."

"Then today you learn." Dottie slapped her thigh, marking her words. "Just tap it against the corner of the counter."

Caitlyn hit it. A squiggly crack appeared around the center of the egg, but it didn't separate.

"Good. Just like that only a little bit harder."

She tried again, adding more force to the motion. The shell shattered and crumbled in her hand, yellow and white oozing between her fingers.

"Not quite so hard."

Dottie was so deadpan in her response that Caitlyn snorted in laughter as she wiped up the mess.

The second attempt proved to be the charm, and soon the filling was whisked and the pie was baking on its 350-degree rack.

They moved through the recipes one at a time, measuring and mixing, sampling and smiling. Hours passed in a cinnamon-scented haven, Dottie letting Caitlyn take the lead and offering her help only as a second-in-command. Somehow, she even coaxed Caitlyn into mixing the meat, egg, and bread crumbs with her own hands. Far too soon the heady aroma of warming meat loaf filled the kitchen, signaling that their afternoon had almost come to an end. Rows of perfect side dishes lined the counter, and all that remained was setting the table with the best china and linen napkins.

Dottie pulled the macaroni and cheese from the oven, resting it on the hot pad next to the stove. Inhaling the smoky spirals coming from crisp edges, she smiled. "I suppose that does it. Just pull the meat loaf out in about forty-five minutes."

Forget garlic angel—Dottie was more like a guardian angel this Christmas. "How can I ever thank you?"

"You're quite welcome, dear. I love cooking."

"But it's so much more than the food. I've barely worried about tonight since you got here. I mean, I've been waking up three times a night for the last week worried I'd spoil dinner. But I haven't even thought about it this afternoon."

Dottie's smile dimmed, her lips pursing. "Why have you been so anxious?"

She couldn't confess the whole truth, could she? Biting her lip, she shook her head. "It's just a big night. First time meeting the parents and all."

"They can't be that scary, can they?"

Caitlyn wound a dish towel around her hands, twisting it until it was almost unrecognizable. With her gaze firmly fixed on an embroidered blueberry, she leaned a hip against the counter. "When I was twenty-five, I dated a guy whose mother didn't approve of me. She said I didn't fit their lifestyle. What she really meant was that I didn't belong to their country club, that the fact that my dad is a plumber and my mom was a teacher was a problem for her."

Dottie slipped the apron strap over her head but made only a low hum encouraging her to continue.

"Brad said he didn't care how his mom felt, but he did. It mattered. Too much." Sniffing back the painful memories, she straightened her shoulders. "He broke up with me about a year later. I'm glad he did, because when I met Ian, I knew I'd never loved anyone like I love him. But if his parents don't like me...I don't think I could handle..." The thought was too hard to say aloud.

"Oh, hon." Dottie's accent kicked in even heavier than usual. "I don't know how anyone could not like you. And it seems to me that the problem with your old boyfriend was his issue, not yours."

Heat rushed to her cheeks. "You're very sweet. But I'm not so sure."

"What is it you're really afraid of?" Dottie held onto her hand, giving it a gentle squeeze.

She pursed her lips and stared at the spot where their hands met, drawing strength from the older woman's sure grip. Just voicing her fear, admitting it, would either give it power or steal its strength. "What if I'm not good enough? I'm thirty-three, and so far no man has thought I'm worth spending his life with. What if there's a reason for that, and Ian just hasn't seen it yet?"

Dottie's eyes squinted as she cupped Caitlyn's cheek with her hand. "What if God has had a plan the whole time? What if He's been preparing both you and Ian for right now? What if this is the first of a lifetime of merry Christmases you'll spend with him? If you live in the awful what-ifs of life, you'll never get to experience the wonderful what-ifs."

Like a cool winter snow, the truth of Dottie's words covered Caitlyn, washing away the fears she'd been holding for so long. The tension in her neck melted, and she inhaled the rich scent of a true holiday meal, one she was proud to serve. One that Dottie deserved to enjoy more than anyone else.

She should invite Dottie to dinner.

The idea struck her with so much force she almost forgot to breathe. Hadn't Dottie's cart been filled with single-serving meals? And she hadn't had anyone else to spend the day with, or she wouldn't have offered to help cook for strangers. Maybe she didn't have a family to share the holiday with. Caitlyn opened her mouth to invite Dottie to stay, but snapped it shut, an image of Ian's disapproving parents flashing across her mind.

What would they say to sharing their traditional dinner with a perfect stranger?

An echo of Dottie's words swept over her. She wouldn't live in fear of the awful what-ifs. Ian's parents might love her and enjoy meeting her new friend. And if they didn't…well, she wasn't going to pretend to be someone she wasn't just to win their approval. That wasn't real approval at all.

The real Caitlyn had just cooked her first meat loaf today. And she wasn't afraid to invite a lonely friend to spend Christmas Eve in her home.

As Dottie slipped an arm into her jacket, Caitlyn strode across the living room.

"Would you like to stay for dinner?"

Dottie tilted her head, her blonde halo flopping to the side, her eyes filled with unspoken questions.

"I know you might already have plans tonight," Caitlyn said quickly, "but it is Christmas Eve. And you've spent all day with me, and you said you didn't have anyone else to spend time with. And you've just been so kind. I'd hate for you to be alone tonight when you put so much into this meal." She paused to take a breath and then let it out in a final burst. "So why don't you join us? You're more than welcome."

Halfway into her coat, Dottie stopped, misty eyes wide and lips pressed tightly together. The tip of her chin quivered, a slow smile illuminating her face. "I have to go. But…thank you. Thank you for opening up your home to me." She turned and vanished as quickly as her whispered words, the door clicking closed behind her.

How strange. She hadn't even said good-bye.

Caitlyn didn't have her phone number or even know her last name. She couldn't count on running into Dottie at the grocery store again, so she chased her outside, flipping on the front light before stepping onto the porch. She surveyed the entire street, even investigating beyond where the road turned. Colorful lights adorned the homes in the neighborhood and cast shadows of Christmas trees and cardboard snowmen. Candy canes lined a neighbor's yard, and someone had added a fiddle to nature's music. But Dottie was nowhere to be found. She'd vanished!

As she traipsed back home, Caitlyn pushed away the sinking feeling that she'd never see her garlic angel again. But there was no time to dwell on that when Ian and his parents would arrive in twenty minutes.

Time flew as she laid out her best dinnerware, tempted to set a place for Dottie. Maybe she would return.

Napkins folded and silver placed, she rushed to change into the right outfit. The suit was too formal, the jeans too casual. She could go through her whole closet and find fault with every piece. So she dressed in her favorite—a red sweater dress with warm brown leggings and cowboy boots. She did live in Nashville, after all. And meeting Southern royalty wasn't going to change that.

She just had to trust that this meeting, this holiday, had been planned long ago.

And now she was ready for it.

When the doorbell rang, her heart leaped. It wasn't fear or anxiety. It was joy—the heart of the season fully realized—that welled deep in her chest. The man she loved was on the other side of her front door, and she ran to meet him and her future in-laws.

What wonderful what-ifs this night could bring.

Ian apparently could not wait to see her either, knocking and opening the door when she was still halfway across the living room. He didn't say anything but let a familiar smile fall into place as he wrapped her in his embrace and pressed a sweet kiss to her cheek. "Merry Christmas Eve, Cait." Before she could pull away and let him offer the introductions, he took a deep breath through his nose. "Smells just like when Mom made it."

"I hope so." Then she stepped back, smoothed down the front of her dress and greeted the man standing behind Ian.

"Caitlyn, this is my dad, James. Dad, this is Caitlyn."

James was the perfect image of Ian thirty years in the future. His hair was still dark, but peppered with wisdom and experience. Lines of laughter curved at the corners of his mouth, his bright teeth white. So this was Augusta's own son, the pride of Georgia.

He reached for her hand and shook it gently, cupping his other hand over the top, drawing her into an emotional embrace. "Caitlyn." He drew out her name like he liked the sound of it. "I am so pleased to know you."

She'd heard that phrase recently. Who else had used that exact wording?

He let go of her hand and stepped to the side as Ian said, "And this is my mom, Judith."

When the petite woman with a halo of blonde curls stepped forward, Caitlyn's breath caught in her throat, and she threw her hands up to her cheeks. "Dottie?"

It couldn't be. She'd opened up her heart to this woman, admitted her very worst fear and confessed her shortcomings. The woman she'd longed to impress had been in her home all day.

Without warning, her future mother-in-law pulled her into a hug that stole the very last bit of her oxygen. And then Dottie whispered into her ear, "I am so very glad that my Ian found you. You're everything I ever hoped for him."

Caitlyn stepped back and glanced between Dottie's smiling face and the confusion reflected on Ian's features.

"I don't understand. You two have met?" Ian's voice caught on a note of disbelief.

Dottie grabbed Caitlyn's hand and squeezed it. "I didn't know who you were when we met at the store, but you looked so lost. I thought I could help. And when you showed me your shopping list, I realized you were cooking our traditional meal at Ian's request. But I didn't want to frighten you."

"So the meals you were buying?"

"Oh, I was just stocking up Ian's refrigerator." Dottie waved her free hand at her son's food choices, her smile never wavering. "I couldn't pass up a chance to really get to know you, to spend time just the two of us. But I didn't mean to mislead you. Forgive me?"

Joy swirled deep inside as Caitlyn nodded in stunned silence. She hadn't lost a friend. She'd gained a mother-in-law. One who already approved of her.

What true angel had been watching over them to make certain that they met at exactly the right time?

Settled in at the table, Caitlyn dished up liberal helpings of meat loaf and fixin's for her guests while Dottie regaled them with stories of Caitlyn's first-time cooking adventures. And as she ate the most delicious meal she'd ever tasted, Caitlyn knew that somehow she'd received so much more than the minor miracle she'd hoped for. This—sharing a meal and celebrating the birth of Christ with loved ones, free from fear— this was a full-scale miracle.

THE BEST DEAD CHRISTMAS TREE

Linda S. Clare

Dressed in my angel wings and the too-big halo, I'm so happy I might fly. All the kids from hospital school are on the elevator, going to the basement for the Christmas pageant rehearsal. There's Sharon and Beatrice, who have cerebral palsy, and Cindy on her crutches.

Who says the Hospital for Children in Salt Lake City, Utah, can't be fun? In the three months I've been here, I've had two operations on my paralyzed arm—the doctors say to make it work better. All the kids here have surgery, but I'm the only patient whose parents live too far away to visit. At least that's what I tell myself. I'm ten, but I keep my white leather Bible under my hospital pillow. I need all the help I can get.

Today I'm excited. After all these months, Mom and Grammie will be here any minute. Mom will play the pageant songs on the piano and then they'll take me home. Home for Christmas! Home is Yuma, Arizona, in case you're wondering.

We don't have snow, but we still have Christmas. And I get to be there! I could fly like an angel.

But then Cindy ruins everything.

She gets a snooty look. She's mad because I'm an angel and she's not. But she's Mary, Jesus's mom, so why is she mad? Maybe Cindy knows the real Mary isn't on crutches, doesn't have a gimpy leg like Cindy does. Doesn't chew her hair like Cindy. I don't know for sure, but my stomach gets that sick feeling when mean Cindy opens her big mouth.

"*My* mommy plays piano too." Cindy twirls the fringe on her Mary shawl. "What's so great about it?"

My face turns hot. Cindy always makes me mad. "I don't see *your* mom here, do I?"

Sharon, her cerebral palsy hands curled up, doesn't say anything. Beatrice looks sad.

Cindy pokes out her lower lip. "That's only 'cause *my* mom just had a baby brother. She'd be here in a minute if she could." Cindy's eyes go squinty. "Do *you* have a brand-new baby brother?"

"No."

"So what took your mom so long to visit?"

Now *my* eyes sting. "My mother's very busy."

Cindy laughs. "I bet she doesn't even want to visit you."

"Liar!" I yell. "Big fat liar!" I hold onto my arm's cast so I won't punch Cindy. The yellow-dress aide, Miss Jensen, says settle down, no yelling.

Sharon looks at me with puppy eyes. I shut up. Inside though, I'm on fire. Hot tears fill my eyes. Cindy pulls her shawl over her face. I can hear her chewing on her hair.

Mom couldn't wait to get here! She planned this visit all along. Mom doesn't hug as much as some moms, but hugs aren't everything. She's beautiful enough for a million hugs. Cindy'll turn green when I wave good-bye in two more days.

The elevator doors pull apart and there's the stage—a manger, pictures of animals, and cardboard palm trees. The hanging aluminum foil star waves in the air conditioning. Jensen pulls Beatrice's bed out of the elevator and drives it right into the wall. She backs up and pushes Sharon to her shepherd's spot.

Cindy whines to the hospital teacher. "Mrs. Andersen." Her eyes dart my way.

Mrs. Andersen holds the fake beards and bath-towel shepherd hats. "Smile, Cindy," she says. "Jesus's mom should smile."

Cindy grins.

"That's the way." Mrs. Andersen tells Cindy to take her place next to the manger. "A beautiful Mary should smile."

A beautiful Mary wouldn't chew her hair, I think. Mrs. Andersen helps Sharon and Beatrice with their costumes and Cindy sticks out her tongue at me. I don't care.

The elevator doors open. Grammie and Mom appear.

Mom looks like Christmas in a gray straight skirt and a red sweater with a green scarf tied around her neck. Her spike heels click on the linoleum. Grammie, dressed in pink with matching pumps, says, "Good morning."

All the patients gather around me. Where'd they come from, how long are they staying? Grammie talks to me and the other kids while Mom thumbs through the sheet music at the piano. I'm the angel but I could be the star the way I'm dancing around. For once this hospital doesn't seem so bad.

Mrs. Andersen gets the boys ready. Grammie waves her arms like the leader of a band. She's a real music teacher, I tell Beatrice.

We take our places. The cattle practice lowing, wise men kneel. Louis, the other one-armed patient who's playing Joseph, yawns and Mary smiles. Shepherds in their beds and fake beards point to the star.

I lift up my good arm and sing. Grammie's arms wave up and down. Mom looks at her music and plays the piano. I wish she'd look at me.

When the first song is over, Mrs. Andersen thanks them. "What a privilege to have you here." She asks Grammie, "How long have you taught music?"

"Going on twenty years," Grammie says. They talk about music and what a cute angel I make. They don't say anything about being a cute one-armed angel.

But Cindy does. In between songs she whispers, "Who ever heard of an angel with a broken wing?"

Louis sticks up for me. "You're just jealous because you're not the angel."

Cindy mutters, "A one-armed angel is so dumb." She wraps her blue Mary shawl tight around her head and shoulders. "You're all so dumb," she hisses from inside the shawl.

Louis is tall but shy. "Hey, I'm one-armed too." He stands over Cindy, his hand on his hip. "Wanna make something of it?"

Cindy stays inside her shawl. If she's crying, it serves her right. I *said* she could be the angel when I go home in two days. Talk about dumb. I concentrate on holding out my arm.

My tinsel halo digs into my forehead. Mrs. Andersen makes us sing "The First Noel" three more times, because Louis keeps singing "*Bald* is the Ki-ing of Israel." Loud as he can. Even Mom chuckles and now nobody thinks Louis is shy. Mrs. Andersen gives him her *attitude adjustment* look.

Finally she wants me to sing "Silent Night." Grammie conducts with her bare arms waggling. My good arm aches from holding it up. I think about the blue spruce Christmas tree we'll pick out, how it'll feel to go back to my old school. At my house in Yuma, all is calm; all is bright. Sleep in heavenly peace.

* * *

I'm counting down the minutes. It's the third day since Mom and Grammie arrived. I'm going home.

My operation was only a few weeks ago, Miss Angelwings says. She's my favorite nurse. I say Mom and Grammie are taking me home. She looks worried.

"Have the doctors said anything about discharge?" Angelwings asks.

I shrug. "Mom says we're going to pick out our Christmas tree." A tiny zing of trouble hits me. "Why else would she and Grammie come all the way here?"

"Maybe to visit?" Miss Angelwings sounds sad.

"Will you write to me in Yuma?"

"Of course." Angelwing's eyes get misty and she goes to the next girl's bed.

Sometimes grown-ups are impossible to figure out.

God isn't easy to understand either. I'm so excited I could tie myself in a bow. I've prayed and thanked and said my fear-not verse a million times, but God is being way too quiet. I feel like shouting, "I'm going home today!" but nobody's paying attention. Mom and Grammie will be here soon, though, and they'll set things straight. You'll see.

* * *

The third day passes. I wake up the next morning and all I see are the usual green spreads on the hospital beds in the big girls' ward. Bed rails and bedpans and bedside tables in a row, twelve girls in all. All of us have bed hair and sleep in our eyes. On the breakfast tray next to my bed, it's lumpy oatmeal, cold toast, and watery juice. Chirpy nurses. The TV's blaring cartoons. It must be Saturday.

My arm doesn't hurt anymore, but the cast's heavy. The operation on my hand must be better by now. Any minute Mom's going to come take me home.

Angelwings smiles. "Picked out a clean dress yet?" Saturdays we get a bath and a clean hospital dress.

Maybe she's asking so the girls who *aren't* leaving won't feel so bad. "Don't need one."

Angelwings says I'm first in line for Saturday bath. My heart trips over itself. That's it!—you have to be clean before you can get on a plane to go home. "Miss Jensen will help you bathe." Angelwings writes something on her clipboard and goes to the next bed.

Jensen? I make the ugliest face. They're letting me go but first I have to take a bath with Jensen? Sharon and Beatrice love my Jensen imitation—her sharp nails dig into our wrists. I pretend to take Sharon's pulse. "Beatrice," I say in a high Jensen voice, "I didn't press hard enough. I'll try harder." The girls laugh, goofy and loud.

Jensen's hands are on her hips and she's not laughing. "All right," she says. My cheeks get warm and I march toward the tub room.

It's dark in here. I climb into the tub. Jensen shuts off the water with an *umph* and scrubs at my skin with a washrag. I don't think I've ever been this clean. But I want to be perfect for my trip home.

I hold my arm cast out of the water. "When do I get this off?" I don't usually talk to Jensen much, but I wasn't planning on going home with this stupid cast.

"How should I know?" Jensen wrings the washrag and wipes my back.

I take deep breaths. "I'm going home today. Don't they cut off your cast first?"

Jensen stops. "Why do you think you're going home?" She squirts shampoo in my hair.

"Mom and my grandmother are here."

Jensen lathers my head, and shampoo trickles into my eyes. "Oh, Susan." Her voice gets softer. "When you're discharged, the chart says 'discharge.' You can't go home until then." She pulls out the sprayer hose. "Close your eyes."

I close them but they pop back open. "Maybe they forgot to write it down. Mom wouldn't come unless I was going home."

"Nobody forgets that kind of thing. Sorry."

Water tumbles over my hair, down my face. Jensen sprays away shampoo; my eyes sting with suds and tears. In my head I plead with God: *please, please.* The roaring sprayer drowns out God's answer.

* * *

Finally, after lunch and rest time, Mom and Grammie come to the ward. My stomach does backflips.

We go to the sun porch. Grammie sits with her back really straight, knees together like a lady. Mom looks funny, like something's wrong, and she crosses one leg over the other. Cross. Uncross. Cross. Maybe it's one of her headaches.

I'm too excited to sit. "When do we leave? Will we get a blue spruce Christmas tree? Where are my clothes?"

Grammie looks at Mom. Mom picks at her thumbnail.

I keep talking. "Sharon gets the orange and pink hot pad I crocheted. Beatrice gets a picture I drew—angels flying over her bed, with my fear-not verse across the top."

Mom says, "Fear not?"

"'And the angel said, "Fear not, for you have found favor with God."'"

"Sweetie." Grammie's acting funny too. I get a stomach zing. "We *thought* the doctors were going to release you before Christmas." There's a tear in her eye.

Mom looks at me as if I just died. "I'm sorry, sweetie."

I stare at the ugly green floor tiles.

Grammie tries to be cheerful. "We're thankful we could come and visit you. You're the prettiest angel." She smiles.

Mom reaches for my hand.

I jump back. "You said we'd pick out a blue spruce tree." I hold my breath to make the tears stay in.

Mom sighs. "I know you're disappointed. We're disappointed too."

Grammie says, "The doctors said it'll only be a little longer. Then you'll be home. You'll see."

"A little longer?" I think about dinosaurs, millions of years of dinosaurs. Is that what she means by a little longer? "Sure." I keep my voice a straight line. "I can wait a little longer."

Grammie pats my shoulder. "That's my girl."

Mom stops crossing her legs. "When you get home we'll have Christmas all over again. How many girls get *two* Christmases?"

I smile but on the inside, I'm shaking hard.

They say good-bye, say over and over that I'll be home in no time. I walk them to the entrance of the ward, smile my famous actress smile and wave until the elevator doors close. Then they're gone.

In the next bed, Sharon smiles but her blue eyes aren't happy—maybe she knows how it feels to be left behind. She clutches my orangey-pink hot pad against her chest.

* * *

That night I stare out the hospital window, scanning for airplanes. If I have to, I'll stare until my eyeballs dry up.

Lights are out on the ward but I sit up in bed. Which lights are stars and which is the plane that holds Grammie and Mom? Airplanes have red lights that blink on and off, I know that much. Stars don't blink. Tonight, they all look the same.

I grip my white Bible until my fingers ache. I looked brave for Grammie and Mom—I don't want them to worry. But now I don't care about Christmas one bit. They can keep all their crummy blue spruce trees.

Navidad, as Beatrice calls it, is in two more days. Cindy says we'll get to do all kinds of Christmassy things—

besides our pageant, which Mom and Grammie won't see, there'll be a turkey dinner, church (probably with Jensen), and Santa and presents. Cindy says the best part will be the parade.

If we go outside for the parade, I'll catch a taxi. I'll tell the driver, "Get me to the airport, and step on it!" I heard it in a movie, but it could work.

The sky gets blacker. So far I haven't seen one single blinking red light. My eyes sting and go droopy. I can't stop yawning. The big clock on the wall is too dark to read.

* * *

On Christmas Eve, it's snowing, the second time I've seen snow. Yuma's in the desert so it never snows. On TV shows like *Bonanza*, Hoss and Little Joe get lost in blizzards. I'd rather have six more surgeries than be lost in a blizzard.

I was right. We have to go to church with Jensen on the sun porch whether we want to or not. A plaster baby Jesus, lying very still in a crèche on the activity table, "was born to save us from our sins," she says. "Don't touch Him. You wouldn't want to break baby Jesus, now would you?"

I look close at the statue, which could fit in my hand. I ask, "Is the plaster the same as our casts?"

"Just don't touch," Jensen says. "Let's sing." She lowers the record player needle. A lady sings Sunday school songs, and the record's *s* sounds like bacon frying. *Sssssss.* Sing, Jensen repeats.

Jensen puts on "Jingle Bells." We sing the funny version: *Jingle Bells, Batman smells, Rudolph laid an egg…* Nurse Jensen scowls, but what can she do? It's Christmas.

Over in one corner of the glassed-in porch, the nurses have decorated a Christmas tree. It's full of droopy branches, lumpy tinsel, and ugly plastic ornaments. It's barely standing up.

In fact, the tree and I are pretty much the only ones able to stand up in this hospital. Besides being the only lucky patient who can walk around, I'm the only one who brought a Bible. I keep it under my pillow. Beatrice prays all the time, but she doesn't have a Bible. How does she expect God to protect her?

While Jensen goes on about cleansing us of our sins, I trace the gold-stamped letters on the front of my King James Version. "What sins do you confess to God?" Jensen asks.

I think of how I hid brussels sprouts from last night's dinner in the drawer of my bedside table. Sharon and Beatrice slipped me theirs too. I wrapped them all in a napkin, but I could still smell them all night long.

"Susan," Jensen repeats, "what do you confess?"

It's easier to lie. "Today I called Sharon a dumb bunny," I say. Right after church I'll flush the sprouts. If God wants the truth, He can ask me Himself.

After lights-out, nobody can sleep. Girls whisper about Santa and how they celebrate Christmas at home. Beatrice says her family goes to midnight mass. Others set out milk and cookies for Santa.

I don't believe this Santa stuff, but I keep quiet. The brussels sprouts were enough trouble for one day. I fall asleep remembering last year's Christmas tree: Daddy laying each piece of tinsel perfectly straight, the smell of the blue spruce in our living room, the angel twinkling on top.

* * *

In the morning we tidy our nightstands and hide the bedpans and throw-up basins. I help the cerebral palsy girls. We make the beds the hospital way: tuck in the green spread all around, fold back the top. No wrinkles.

I'm too excited to care if my spread's wrinkled. Time for the parade!

And I may just explode! I can't wait to open the presents I asked Mom and Daddy for: Nancy Drew mystery books and a Madame Alexander collector's doll—one from France will suit me fine. Then I frown. Most of the girls have casts on their legs and can't wear shoes. When we go outside to watch the parade, how will they keep their feet warm? I smile some more—the nurses must have thought of something.

Jensen comes on duty. "Be on your best behavior," she says, "so Santa will visit the ward." She looks right at me. "But for your safety, stay on your beds."

Beatrice says, "When are we going outside?"

Jensen looks confused. "Who said you're going outside?"

Everyone yells, "For the parade!"

"Parade?" Jensen's eyes go soft. She shakes her head slowly. "You'll have to watch from your beds." Her shoes squeak fast as she practically runs out to the nurse's station.

Everyone's mouth hangs open. Someone starts to cry. The girls' ward is three stories up, and our beds are nowhere near the windows. Everyone gets quiet.

When the coast is clear, I sneak off my bed and go to the window. Down on the parking lot, a bunch of Saint Nicks look up and wave. "Santas!" I point. "And clowns! Big old clowns riding on tricycles!" I jump up and down in my socks.

The Santas yell, "Merry Christmas." From up here, they look like Santa ants.

Jensen squeaks back in. "Back on your bed, Susan." I climb onto my bed like the other girls. We wait for Santa. We wait a long time.

At home Daddy always makes my little sister Sandy and me brush our teeth before we're allowed to see what Santa brought. Two sips of hot chocolate and a bite of cinnamon roll. Then presents, one at a time.

By now my sister has probably torn off all the wrapping paper, squealed over all the toys. She's probably already wrecked the hairdo on her new doll and spilled hot chocolate on her good pajamas. Mom's busy cooking. Dad's staring at his perfect Christmas tree icicles. I can almost smell home.

Just before lunch, Santa shows up carrying a big red sack. He wears motorcycle boots just like Daddy's and too much aftershave. His "ho ho ho" could use some work.

Cindy oohs and aahs over everything. Sharon's eyes shine. Beatrice asks me, "What did you ask Santa to bring you?"

I don't answer.

Motorcycle Santa passes out two wrapped gifts to every girl. They let our mommies and daddies send presents! My heart pounds faster.

Santa finally comes to me. "Ho, ho, ho," he says. "Have you been a good little girl?"

"I'm in fourth grade," I say. "That's not little."

Santa reaches inside his sack and fishes out two gifts. "Meeeerry Christmas," he says. His fake white beard looks soft as a palomino mane.

I clutch my packages. "Thank you, Santa," I say, but he's already moved on.

I look at my gifts. Wait a minute. These aren't from anyone I know. My heart goes numb. I read the tag: Merry Christmas, for a Girl. I stare at the box. These gifts are from strangers.

Beatrice can't open hers, so I help. She got a pale-skinned doll and a ballpoint pen. Don't they know Beatrice can barely write her name?

I turn back to my presents, tear away the paper. Rochelle the Southern Belle, the tag says. She is a plastic doll dressed in pale blue lace. She isn't from India or France. I shove her aside. The other box holds a stuffed reindeer wearing a Rudolph cartoon smile. I swallow, scoop up the gifts, and run.

Someone's made a big mistake! I'm the only patient who can run to find Santa. My socks slip on the linoleum. At the ward door, Jensen grabs my shoulders. "Slow down. Where are you going?"

I twist away, but her fingernails dig in. "I've got to talk to Santa." My voice catches. "We got the wrong presents. Santa gave us the wrong presents."

Motorcycle Santa and his helpers stuff themselves into the elevator. The doors glide together. They're gone.

Jensen frowns. "Not all the patients come from nice homes. Some of the children are disadvantaged. We don't want anyone to feel bad." She leads me back toward the ward and stops at my bed. "It's been a pretty long day. Maybe you need to rest a little?"

A wave of tiredness crashes onto my head. I nod like I'm dead and climb onto my smooth green spread. I lie back on my pillow, hug my good arm across my stomach, and close my eyes.

* * *

For supper we get turkey and trimmings. Nobody eats much. All evening long Beatrice whispers in Spanish, tears dripping off her chin. The night nurse can't figure out what's wrong.

After lights-out I sneak out of bed and tiptoe out to the sun porch. Baby Jesus is still in the crèche with His arms outstretched. It's not allowed, but I lift Him from His manger and hold Him gently. He's only plaster but somehow Jesus makes me feel better. Maybe He won't mind spending the night with me.

Before the nurses come by on bed check, I curl Beatrice's fingers around baby Jesus and climb back into my bed. She stops crying. I'll put Jesus back before Jensen comes on duty.

Out the window, snow keeps falling. The ward's quiet. I reach under my pillow for my Bible. Beatrice finally falls asleep clutching the Savior, but His arms reach out to me.

* * *

It's the third week in January and I'm still in the hospital. I should be grateful, though. Some of the patients have been here forever.

The ones with casts from their toes up to their chins say it takes a whole year to get discharged. The cast starts out chin to toes, then after six months they cut the plaster legs off so the cast stops at their hips. Later, the body cast girls say, they get a metal brace that keeps their chin up and their back straight. They have to wear their brace all day, even at recess. Jumping rope sounds impossible. How will they see their feet?

If we had jump rope here, I'd be the only jumper. But sometimes at school in Yuma they won't let me play double Dutch. You need two hands to turn double. I never thought I'd find anything good about this hospital, but there it is—at least nobody laughs because you can't turn two ropes at the same time.

But I miss the way the hot wind lifts up your skirt in Yuma. I miss my bedroom and my teacher and Bible class, although I'm way behind on memory verses. I miss my own bed and my own clothes. I hope they miss me too.

Jensen blows into the ward with a clipboard and a scowl. She takes Beatrice's wrist. Jensen complains about no over-time pay and how much work the nurses pile on the aides. Her lips move while she counts the pulse. She scribbles on the clipboard, then looks at Beatrice. "Time for PT." She lowers Beatrice's bed rail.

Beatrice makes a face. Everybody knows she's afraid of physical therapy. "Do I have to?" She looks worried.

"Yep." Jensen brings a wheelchair around to the side of the bed and helps Beatrice into the seat. "Let's go!" Jensen says and fastens the seat belt. It's too tight. I can tell.

I slide off my bed and stand in front of Jensen. "Loosen her belt, okay? She can't breathe." I give Beatrice a look that says don't worry.

Jensen looks at me like she's annoyed, but then she smiles. "Susan. I'll be back to get you in a minute." She pushes Beatrice's wheelchair toward the ward entrance. Beatrice stares back at me until they round the corner.

After a while, Jensen comes back. "Where's Beatrice?" I ask. Maybe I'll see my friend in PT. I'll help her climb the stairs that go nowhere.

"Get your things together," Jensen says.

"What things?"

"Clean out your nightstand." She's smiling like she just won on *Queen for a Day*.

I open my bedside drawer and take out my Nancy Drew books, those dumb Christmas presents, and my stationery. "Where's Beatrice?" I ask again.

By now nosy Cindy is butting in. "Miss Jensen," Cindy whines. She brushes her cheek with a curl of her chewed-up hair—swish, swish, back and forth. "Miss Jensen?"

Jensen shakes her head. "Not now, Cindy. I'm busy."

"But, Miss Jensen..."

"Cindy," Jensen sighs, "I'm afraid you'll have to wait."

I look at Cindy, and mouth two words: *shut up*.

"Got your things?" Jensen's checking my nightstand.

"Where are we going?" I reach under my pillow for my Bible.

Cindy sticks out her tongue. I smile a big fake smile.

"You'll see." Jensen fills a paper sack with my books, stationery, some school papers, Bible, and my Christmas gifts, Rochelle the Southern Belle and Rudolph. She leads me out of the ward.

We go to the closet where the patients' belongings are stored. Jensen pulls down the box marked with my name in big black letters. It's all still there: red dress, princess coat, new socks, slip, and undies. In the cast room I take off my hospital dress, let it drop to my ankles. I'm in my underwear but I don't care. My heart pounds louder and jet planes roar through my ears. Could it be? Could it really be?

Before I can put on my dress, a doctor comes in. His white coat is long, down past his knees. He doesn't say much but he's dreamy like Dr. Kildare on TV. He smiles and says I'm a pretty girl. My face gets red-hot and now I wish I wasn't half-naked.

I get up onto the cold table. He cuts off the cast. Then he makes me do stuff with my bad hand: raise your wrist, touch your fingers with your thumb, make a V for victory, the sign for A-okay. It's hard but I do my best.

"Looks like this is your lucky day." Dr. Kildare pats my hand and my neck prickles at the touch.

"My lucky day?" I can't believe it. Am I really going home?

"Be good." Dr. Kildare shakes my good hand and we say good-bye.

My red dress barely fits now—the top buttons won't close. Guess I can't wear it back in Yuma.

I'm worried about Beatrice and Sharon. "Can we go back to the ward so I can tell everyone good-bye?" How will they do things if I'm not there to help?

"Sorry, the taxi's waiting." Jensen leads me into the elevator. Just like that, the big girls' ward is gone.

Down at the hospital's main entrance the whole world has been going on without me. I feel like an Egyptian mummy that's come back to life. A chaperone says the taxi driver is waiting.

I shove my paper bag into the chaperone's hands. "But I have to say good-bye to Sharon and Beatrice. It'll only take a minute." I tug off my coat and hand it to her. "One minute's all I need."

The chaperone looks sad. "We have to leave immediately." She gives me back my coat.

"But no one told me I was leaving!"

She opens the heavy glass doors anyway. "Come along now, or we'll miss our flight."

I plead with Jensen. "Can't you do something?"

Jensen sighs.

"Will you say good-bye to Beatrice and Sharon for me? Will you?"

"Sure." What if Jensen forgets? Before I can say anything else, Jensen's gone back inside. The chaperone's waiting to take me home.

Home. Sometimes you have to decide. I slide across the cab's brown plastic seat.

Pictures of this hospital world zip through me: Sharon and Beatrice as shepherds in their beds, Cindy whining, Louis sticking up for me. The school teacher and Angelwings. "Good-bye, good-bye, good-bye!"

* * *

Phoenix Sky Harbor Airport looks brown with roads going out like the spokes of a bicycle wheel. Around the airport are green fields as far as I can see. On the edges of the fields gray-green palo verde and cactus lift up their branches. The plane bumps hard, and we're down.

At the bottom of the plane's stairs, a roar comes from everywhere at once. The sun's too bright and it's way too hot here. Lots of people stand at the gate, tons of nobody-I-know leaning on the chain-link fence. My insides grab. What if they forgot to tell Mom? I hunt for something I know, listen for sounds I remember.

Then I hear Mom yell, "No!" My little sister runs toward me, her back to the sun, curly light hair bouncing with the wind. She squeezes through the gate and throws her arms around me.

The next thing is hugs and everyone talking at once. I get kisses from Grammie. Daddy wears a red polo shirt and jingles the change in his pockets. I strip off my coat. After all these months, home is browner and hotter than I remember. I suck in a gulp of Arizona air and let the sun hit my face.

Daddy says we'll drive all night through the desert to get to Yuma. We leave when the sky is purple, when the stars are barely twinkling. The car windows are down and we sing "Waltzing Matilda" and "Ninety-Nine Bottles of Beer on the Wall." I lie on my side and stare up at the stars. Orion marches along with us, as if God told him to walk me home.

I close my eyes and open them again. It's still night, but presto, there's our carport, our brown house, our sweet peas trailing up the front. It's shivery, dark, and cold, and for a moment I wish I were still wearing my coat.

Daddy leads me to the living room and switches on the lights.

My mouth hangs open. Right next to the picture window is a tall blue spruce Christmas tree, complete with lights and decorations and an angel on top. Underneath, on the bed-sheets that are supposed to look like snow, piles of presents sit, wrapped and topped with bows.

The tree isn't blue anymore, though. It's totally dead. The needles are petrified brown, and they drop off if you even breathe. Skinny branches droop where the ornaments pull them down and all the wires for the lights show. The poor tree looks naked and really, really old. It must have stood there since before Christmas. It's the most beautiful dead Christmas tree ever.

Mom comes in and smiles at me. "We wanted you to have Christmas with us," she says. "We left everything until you came home."

Christmas at the end of January sounds good to me.

Daddy hands me a present. I tear into it and pull out a Madame Alexander doll. She's from France, in a black maid's outfit with a white apron and hat. I hold her close, shut my eyes, and breathe in. Dead Christmas tree smell mixes with Mom's perfume. The angel on the top blinks on and off, saying she's been with me all along.

BENEATH THE
CHRISTMAS STAR

Johnnie Alexander Donley

December 1944
Bradford County, Florida

Jimmy Fuller lightly scraped his knife blade along the pale grain of the dolphin he was shaping from an orange-tree branch. Wooden shavings and broken pieces, his earlier failed attempts, littered the scarred table. He couldn't mess up again. Not if Ma was going to have a present under the Christmas tree.

Static interfered with the familiar carols playing on the radio. Perched on a nearby stool, Polly Grant munched one of the cookies she'd brought over for him.

Jimmy narrowed his eyes, focusing on the sharp blade as the shavings peeled away to reveal the dolphin's dorsal fin. When the sides appeared even, he placed the dolphin on his palm and held it up for inspection.

"Finally." He let out a deep breath. "What do you think?"

Polly examined the wooden figure and then looked up at him. "It's perfect."

"Not as good as Pa can do." Jimmy rifled through a shallow box, running several scraps of sandpaper through his fingers before choosing one.

"Your ma will love it just as much."

"I hope so."

"Have you heard from your pa yet?"

The concern in Polly's voice squeezed Jimmy's stomach. He shook his head.

"That doesn't mean anything bad has happened. We got two letters from my pa after he…" Polly's voice cracked and she sniffed. "The mail can be awfully slow from over there."

Jimmy bent his head, intent on sanding the dolphin's underbelly. But he couldn't stop the memory of finding Polly down by Canoe Creek after the military men had made the dreaded visit to her house. Nothing he'd said consoled her. In all his twelve years, he'd never felt so useless.

Since then, he found himself cringing every time a vehicle pulled into their dirt lane.

He gently blew away the sawdust created by the sandpaper and rubbed the smooth spot with his thumb. Pa's last letter had come weeks ago, right before Thanksgiving. He couldn't tell them where he was, but Jimmy had studied the big European map at school. Polly's pa died on D-day, struggling to get ashore at Normandy. Jimmy's pa was in the same unit, so he had to be somewhere in France. Maybe even in Germany.

An involuntary shudder ran up Jimmy's spine. "Stupid war," he murmured under his breath. If only he was older, taller. He'd lie about his age and join up. He'd make those Germans pay for killing Polly's dad. For ruining their lives.

As if she'd read his mind, Polly sighed. "I wish there'd never been a war. That everything was like it used to be."

"No good wishin' for things that can't be."

"Then I wish your pa would come home soon." She jumped down from her stool and wandered over to the radio.

Jimmy stared at her back as she fiddled with the knobs. A thick blonde braid tied with scraps of blue ribbon nearly reached her waist. She'd never cried in front of him again, not since that first time. Not even at the funeral. But she'd changed. The old Polly was like a mason jar filled to the brim with fireflies, all bright and cheerful. Seemed like now the jar was empty.

Polly shifted the radio antenna, and Bing Crosby's voice broke through the static. The familiar words of "White Christmas" filled the workshop.

Jimmy carefully set the dolphin on its oval base and slid from his stool. "Wish we could have a white Christmas."

Polly faced him, rewarding his teasing with a dimpled smile that made his stomach do a weird flip-flop. "Wouldn't it be fun to make a snowman?"

"Not gonna happen as long as we live around here." He grabbed a cookie and stuffed half of it into his mouth.

"What do you suppose it feels like? Snow?"

"Cold."

"I'd like to see a white Christmas."

"Someday I'll make sure you do."

"Promise?"

Jimmy held out his little finger. "Pinky swear."

Polly crooked her little finger in his. "Pinky swear."

The rumble of a motor interrupted the solemn ceremony.

They both peered through the workshop window as a sheriff's vehicle parked before the frame house. Jimmy's chest tightened, and his shoulders tensed.

Polly grasped his arm. "It's not the army," she said, her soothing voice tinged with fear.

"C'mon." Jimmy headed for the door, Polly close behind him. By the time they got outside, the deputy was standing by his car and looking around. Jimmy's ma, wiping her hands on her apron, stepped through the kitchen door and onto the porch.

"Hello, Deputy Wilkes," she called out. "What brings you out our way?"

"Miz Fuller." The deputy tipped his hat above a plump face lined and tanned by all the days he'd spent in the Florida sun. "I just dropped by to check on you and your place."

Jimmy joined Ma, and she gave him a hesitant smile. Sauntering toward them, Deputy Wilkes eyed the children as if sizing them up. "Hello, Jimmy. Polly."

They returned his greeting, then Ma offered him a cup of coffee. "Bit chilly even for December, isn't it?"

"Sure is," said Deputy Wilkes. "And I sure appreciate the offer, but I don't have the time."

"Is something wrong, deputy?"

He pressed his lips together, then exhaled heavily. "I don't like sayin' anything in front of the young 'uns, but I reckon they need to know."

"Know what?" Jimmy blurted. Ma put her hands on his shoulders, and he resisted the urge to shrug them away. With

Pa gone, the farm was his responsibility. Whatever Deputy Wilkes had to say, Jimmy didn't need his ma to baby him.

"One of them German POWs from over at Camp Blanding escaped this morning."

Behind Jimmy, Ma gasped. Polly's eyes widened and she covered her mouth with her hands.

Impatience rattled Jimmy's composure, but he stuck his hands on his hips and thrust out his chest. "Well, he better not come here. Not iffen he wants to live."

"Shh," Ma said, giving him a small shake. "None of that talk now."

Deputy Wilkes smiled. "The boy's got the right spirit, ma'am. Why we gotta take care of those Nazis is beyond me. I hear tell they eat better than some of our own folks."

"How did he escape?" Ma used her change-the-subject voice, but Jimmy wanted to hear more of the deputy's opinions. He didn't understand why the POWs were here, either. They were the ones to blame for taking men from their farms and fathers from their children. To Jimmy, they deserved to be locked up—or worse.

"Not sure. But it's hard to think he got too far. Seems he was beaten up pretty bad."

"Beaten up?" Ma's horrified voice rose in pitch.

"Was the other POWs, not our boys. Some kind of political argument, from what the brass were saying. Makes no sense to me."

"Nor to me."

"Well, I just stopped by to give you the news. The army didn't want it broadcast on the radio, but the sheriff, he says folks have a right to know. So you can be on guard an' all."

"We'll be careful, deputy. Thank you."

"Polly, I'm stoppin' at your place next. Maybe I should take you on home."

Polly opened her mouth to protest, but Ma spoke first. "That's a good idea. Thank you, deputy. Polly, please tell your mother we'll expect you both for Christmas dinner tomorrow."

"As long as that ol' German doesn't murder us all in our sleep," Jimmy muttered.

"He won't, will he?" Polly asked, her eyes round.

"No," Ma said with finality. She gave Jimmy a stern look. "I'm sure he'll be back in the camp in no time. Isn't that right, deputy?"

"That's right, ma'am. In no time at all. He might even be back there right now."

As the deputy scanned the homestead and surrounding landscape, Jimmy followed his gaze to see the farm as the deputy must be seeing it. His face reddened as he noted the peeling paint on the house, the crooked fence posts and loose boards enclosing the empty corral. The hedgerow separating the home place from the fields and groves needed clearing and trimming. If Pa came home—no, *when* he came home, Jimmy scolded himself—he might not even recognize the place.

"See you tomorrow, Jimmy." Polly stood by the rear door of the deputy's car. "Merry Christmas."

"Merry Christmas," he said dully. He and Ma watched them drive away.

"Come on into the house now," Ma said.

"I still have stuff to do in the workshop."

"You'll have to do it in the house."

"Ma," Jimmy protested.

"Gather what you need." Ma crossed her arms, peering nervously around the farm. "I'll wait for you."

In the workshop, Jimmy put the dolphin on the plate of cookies and covered it with the cloth Polly had left.

"Hurry up," Ma called.

"Comin'!" Grabbing his sandpaper, he rushed out the door. Just like a Nazi to ruin Christmas Eve.

* * *

Kurt Richter waded in the tea-colored water of the shallow stream, sticking close to the tree-lined bank. Cypress trees emerged from the water, their thick branches crisscrossing above his head and trapping cool breezes that raised goose bumps on his arms and legs. He paused near a cypress knee that protruded from the stream and leaned against its rough bark.

Slapping his arms to restore circulation, he glanced around, alert for any sign of pursuit. The gurgling of the stream as it flowed around the tree and across the sandy bottom calmed his breathing. Out here, in this strange tropical wilderness, there was no sign of civilization. He might be the first man to ever walk this stream.

But danger could not be that far behind. His sanctuary was only an illusion.

Closing his eyes, he lifted his face to the sky. The afternoon sun filtered through the canopy of leaves above him, dappling his bruised features with light and warmth.

"Show me where to go, Father," he whispered in German. "Lead my footsteps."

A chill gust of wind swept along the stream, ruffling his short hair and biting his fingers.

"*Brr.*" He rubbed his hands together, then chuckled. On his faraway farm, cows had needed to be milked, livestock needed to be fed no matter how deep the snow or how harsh the winter winds screaming down the mountains. "You laugh at me, *Gott,* that this little wind shivers me. I laugh too that this is so."

He pushed away from the tree's bump, trudging through the ankle-high water despite the aching coldness in his feet and the agony that gripped his ribs. He followed the stream for several miles until it curved back on itself.

Leaving the stream, he struck out on a zigzag course through palmettos and scrubs, into a stand of pines and hardwoods. On the other side, he discovered an orderly grove. The orange trees, their branches weighed down with their golden fruit, stretched in neat rows. Yielding to his hunger, he yanked an orange from the nearest tree and sat beneath it. After pulling the thick peel from the juicy sections, he popped them into his mouth.

A grove meant people, but there was no telling what kind. In the few months, he'd been at the POW camp he'd learned that the Americans weren't much different from the *Volk* back home. Several of the guards were good-natured, easy-going men. The two on duty at the road project didn't pay much attention to the prisoners under their watch. He'd had no trouble slipping away from the arduous chore of clearing the scrub.

Other Americans were brusque, like the foreman at the sugarcane fields near Clewiston. Caring more about money than men, he saw the German POWs as cheap labor to be worked till they dropped. He subconsciously rubbed his ribs. One good thing about the beating he'd endured: it got him sent away from the Clewiston camp and back to Camp Blanding.

He ate a second orange and wiped his hands on his pants. Somehow he needed to find a change of clothes. Anyone living around here would recognize the uniform as that of the POWs, but even if they didn't, the large white *P* and *W* on the back of his shirt gave him away.

What kind of people cared for this grove?

He hoped he could get different clothes without finding out.

Keeping close to a line of trees, he walked through the grove. A few minutes later, he saw a thin stream of white smoke as if from a chimney. Someone had a fire going, from a fireplace or a cookstove, and it wasn't that far away. He headed that direction, alert to any strange sounds.

A shabby hedge separated the grove from the homestead. The low house, with its wraparound porch and metal roof, formed a triangle with the two worn outbuildings. He crouched behind the brush and prayed that whoever lived there didn't own a dog.

All appeared quiet, but he was certain someone was in the house. As he wavered on what to do, the screen door opened. A woman and a boy came out of the house. Richter leaned forward, staring at the woman. She wore a man's jacket over a print housedress and rubber boots. Her brunette hair was swept above her neck in a loose bun. *The woman with the broken car.*

Shortly after he'd arrived in Florida, he was on a work detail near where the woman's car had stalled beside the road. The American guards couldn't fix it, so Richter had volunteered. A few minutes fiddling under the hood, and the engine had roared to life. She'd given him half a dozen fresh eggs in gratitude.

Now she turned her head from one side to the other, her posture alert and watchful. Together she and the boy entered the barn, leaving the door wide open. A cow mooed from inside.

As Kurt hid behind the hedge, the woman and boy completed their tasks and returned to the house. The sun cast long shadows as dusk fell. In the twilight, Kurt considered his options. The barn animals might alert the woman to his presence. But neither she nor the boy had gone into the other building. Perhaps he could shelter there till morning.

He took the long way around and slipped through the door. After a few moments, his eyes adjusted to the darkness and he looked around the workshop. A lantern, about half-filled with oil, rested in a nook in the wall. He brushed away cobwebs and lit the wick.

The weak light revealed a workshop with a bench and tools along one wall, stools, even a radio. On the bench, he found several pieces of raw wood and whittled shapes. He picked up a half-formed dolphin with a broken fin.

A knife lay among the shavings, and he ran his thumb along the blade. A sharp weapon might come in handy.

In the far corner, he found a chest containing assorted gear and horse blankets. He pulled a couple out, inhaling the familiar smell, and curled up in a corner. Memories of Christmases on his own farm with his own family haunted him as he drifted to sleep, the knife secure in his grasp.

* * *

Jimmy polished the wooden dolphin from snout to tail with a soft cloth. Now all he had to do was wrap his present and place it under the tree. He smiled, imagining Ma's face when she opened her gift. Not as good as anything Pa could do, but not bad either.

He plopped on his bed and placed the dolphin in the middle of a colorful page he'd torn from a magazine. Gathering the corners together with a red ribbon Polly had given him, he managed a crooked bow and frowned. If only he'd finished the dolphin sooner so Polly could have helped him with the wrapping.

A not-too-bad present in not-that-great wrapping.

Ma deserved better.

He leaned back against his pillow and clenched his fist as frustration roiled his stomach. Nothing was as it should be. Not with Pa gone.

What if he never comes back?

The unbidden question sickened him. It seemed disloyal somehow, and eerily powerful, as if putting his fear into words could make it come true.

A knock sounded on his door. "Jimmy?" Ma's gentle voice drifted into his room. "The Christmas Eve program is about to come on."

"I'll be out in a minute."

"Hurry. Popcorn's on the stove."

As Jimmy sat up, her soft footsteps receded down the hall. For some reason, they had to go through the motions as if this was a Christmas like all the ones before the war. Eating popcorn and listening to the radio broadcast of the Nativity story. Going outside to search for the Christmas star. Singing "Silent Night" before going to bed.

The familiar traditions sharpened Pa's absence, but somehow eased it too. Wherever Pa was, he'd know what they were doing at home. He'd know how much they missed him.

Jimmy picked up his wrapped dolphin and headed for the living room. In the kitchen, popping corn pinged against the pot's metal lid and filled the house with its familiar warmth.

The Christmas tree, a five-foot pine he and Ma had cut from the woods behind the house, stood in front of the curtained picture window. Homemade ornaments, fragile balls, and strands of brightly colored lights adorned the fragrant branches. He placed his gift beside the two packages his grandparents had sent them.

Probably clothes.

He pasted on a grin before entering the kitchen. "Smells good, Ma."

"Almost ready." She beamed a too-bright smile at him as she shook the covered saucepan above the burner. Her red-rimmed eyes glistened. "Do you want to pour the cocoa?"

"Sure." Jimmy pulled two mugs from the cupboard. "What about butter for the popcorn?"

"Melting on the back burner." Ma gave the saucepan a final shake, and the white kernels cascaded into a large bowl. "All done."

Within a few minutes, they were settled in their favorite spots in front of the big radio. Ma sat in her cushioned rocker, and Jimmy sprawled on the floor in front of the fireplace with two large pillows. He pulled a maple limb from the kindling basket and studied it. Might make a snowflake for Polly. If he started on it now, he could give it to her tomorrow at dinner. He shoved his hand into his pocket, but it was empty.

"I left my knife in the workshop," Jimmy said, waving the limb. "Can I run out and get it so I can whittle something?"

"The program is about to start. You can get it in the morning."

Morning would be too late. "I'll get it when we go out to look for the Christmas star."

A shadow crossed Ma's face. "I don't think we should look for the star this year."

Jimmy's eyes about popped out of his head. He couldn't remember a Christmas when they hadn't gone out to search the sky, not even when he was five and a late tropical storm blew across the peninsula from the Atlantic to the Gulf. Pa had bundled him in a tarp and carried him out into the bleak night to find the star that had guided the wise men to Jesus's home in Bethlehem.

'Course it wasn't the real Christmas star. But every year, the Fuller family picked out the brightest star in the night sky as their special way to celebrate Jesus's birth.

Jimmy had never forgotten how safe he'd felt in Pa's strong arms even as the wind tried to whip the tarp from his body and the rain blew into his eyes. He clung to Pa as he lifted his face to the heavens in search of the brightest star. On that wild night, the stars hid behind black clouds...except for one pin-point of light that somehow pierced the darkness. Ma quickly dubbed it the Christmas star, and they all ran back to the house, drenched to the skin and doubling over with laughter.

Seemed kind of silly now. But what he wouldn't give to know that Pa was remembering that night too.

"But we have to," he said. "We always look for the star."

"It might not be safe," Ma said. Jimmy followed her gaze to the front door. Ma had locked and bolted it as soon as Deputy Wilkes and Polly had left. When it came time for evening chores, she'd insisted they stay together to milk the cow, feed the pigs, and close up the chickens in their coop. Just a precaution, she'd said. She hadn't been too happy when Jimmy shut himself in his room to varnish and wrap her present.

"I'm not afraid of any ol' German goose-stepper."

"Hush now. You know I don't like that kind of talk, Jimmy." Ma fingered the popcorn kernels in the bowl on her lap. "It's unkind."

"It's what he is."

"*What* he is?" Ma shook her head. "We know nothing about him. Except that he's far from home. Like your pa."

"He'd be nothin' like my pa. And he better not show his face on our place."

"I doubt we have anything to worry about."

"Then why can't we look for the star?"

"Let's just enjoy the radio program, shall we? Turn up the sound a bit."

Jimmy ate his popcorn without really tasting it as the announcer read the familiar words from the second chapter of the Gospel of Luke. Hymns and Christmas carols alternated with a variety of sketches—some funny, some serious. Ma tried to sing along with the first song, but her voice cracked, and she gave up halfway through it. She didn't sing another.

The absence of her sweet alto voice made it even harder for Jimmy to sit through the program.

As the hour hand approached nine, Jimmy became more fidgety. When the show ended, he got to his feet. "Wherever Pa is, he'll be looking up at the sky for the Christmas star right now, 9 PM our time. We got to be looking for it too."

Ma sat her popcorn bowl at her feet. It was still nearly full. "I just don't think—"

"But, Ma." Jimmy grabbed his jacket off the hook near the door and slipped it on. "It's tradition. We can't be the ones to break it. Not when Pa's not even here."

Ma gazed at him, her gray eyes filled with sadness. "I only want to keep you safe."

"I know, Ma." Jimmy reached for her hand. "Please, let's go outside. Just a little ways."

He could tell by the look in her eyes, the tilt of her head, that she was wavering. "For Pa's sake."

She glared at him, but one corner of her mouth turned upward. "Not fair."

"C'mon. Please."

She let him pull her from the chair and lead her to the door. "Only a few minutes, you understand?"

"Understand."

She unlocked and unbolted the door, then peered into the night before turning on the porch light. Jimmy followed her outside to the broad expanse between the house and the out-buildings.

"It's breezy out here," she said, rubbing her arms.

"Wonder what it's like wherever Pa is."

"Probably much colder. Maybe even snowing."

"Have you ever seen snow, Ma?"

"Once. I wasn't much older than you when my family went north for the holidays. I'd never been so cold in my life."

"Did you make a snowman?"

"Yes. And went ice-skating."

Jimmy shook his head. It all sounded so strange. If not for pictures in his books or wintry scenes at the picture show, he'd never believe such a thing possible as a frozen pond.

"Let's find the star," Ma said, interrupting his thoughts. "Which one is the brightest?"

"One to the north," Jimmy said. "That's where Pa is probably looking."

"I think he might look southwest. Towards us." Ma's familiar lilt had returned to her voice. She took him gently by the shoulders and shifted him. "So let's look more east. This way."

Jimmy stared into the dark sky. A multitude of stars twinkled among the few clouds that moved slowly across the heavens. "That one," he said, pointing to a large point of light.

"I believe you're right."

"I hope Pa picks that one too."

"He will. I'm sure of it." She squeezed his shoulders. "Let's go back in now."

"I need to get my knife first." Jimmy shrugged from her grasp and headed for the workshop.

"Can't it wait till morning?" Ma called after him.

"'Take care of your tools, and they'll take care of you,'" he shouted back, quoting one of Pa's favorite sayings. "Besides, I wanna make something for Polly."

She smiled broadly, seeming to relax for the first time since Deputy Wilkes had showed up, then followed him to the workshop.

* * *

The sound of voices in the clear night stirred Richter from his fitful sleep. As he rose to his feet, the door opened and the overhead light brightened the room. He blinked, instinctively crouching into a fighting position, the blade held outward as he shaded his eyes with his other hand to see the intruder.

"You!" The boyish voice sounded more surprised than scared.

Kurt blinked again as the boy wheeled around and raced out the door. "Jimmy," called a woman's voice. She appeared in the doorway, and they stared at each other. "I've seen you before."

Taking a deep breath, Richter relaxed his grip on the knife and lowered his hand to his side. "You were kind to me."

"Because you fixed my car." Doubt and worry flitted across her features. "You're the one who escaped."

He ducked his head in acknowledgment. *"Ja."*

She stared at the knife, and he let it fall to the floor. "I mean no harm," he said, spreading his hands. "I only needed a place to stay."

"The deputy said you were beaten. By the other prisoners."

He gingerly touched his bruised cheek and shrugged. "A misunderstanding."

"About what?"

"I am loyal to my country as it was, not to the man they call *der Fuhrer.*" He held her gaze, willing her to see he told the truth. "For this, I am named a traitor by those who follow Hitler."

"And you don't?"

He opened his mouth, wanting to explain that not all Germans were Nazis, when the boy burst through the door, a rifle in his hands.

"Move, Ma!" he ordered.

The next seconds were a blur as the boy raised the rifle to his shoulder. The woman stepped between them, her arms outspread in front of Kurt, who backed up against the wall.

"Get outta the way, Ma," he said, his voice shaking. Angry tears filled his eyes, and the boy brushed them away with a swipe of his sleeve.

"Jimmy! Don't do this," she said. "It'd be murder."

"They killed Polly's dad." Jimmy's voice broke, and he tightened his grip on the rifle. "And who knows what they've done with Pa."

"This man has done nothing to your pa, Jimmy."

Richter sidestepped so the woman no longer shielded him, but she shifted with him. "You need not protect me," he said. "I will not hide behind a woman."

She whirled to face him, hands on her hips. "It's him I'm protecting," she said, pointing over her shoulder to her boy. "He will not carry your death on his conscience."

Her words sifted into his mind along with images of his own son, whom he hadn't seen in three years. "I never wished to fight. Only to farm, as you do here. With my cows and my pigs." He blinked away the hot tears that burned his eyelids.

* * *

Jimmy glared at the German, his breath quick and shallow, causing a pain in his chest. His finger rested against the trigger, but the sweat coating his palms made it difficult to hold the rifle steady.

The German picked up a block of wood from the bench. "I only wish this war to end so I may go home to my wife and my son. To teach him to work with his hands as you do. To make things, not destroy."

A strange feeling shot up Jimmy's spine. The German's words sounded so much like something his father would have said. He tamped the feeling down, summoning his rage.

"I'm Irene Fuller," Ma said, unexpectedly extending a hand. "This is my son, Jimmy."

"Kurt Richter." The German gingerly took her hand, clicked his heels together, and bowed. "I am pleased to meet you, Frau Fuller. Herr Fuller."

"You are welcome to spend the night here, Mr. Richter." Ma turned to Jimmy and held out her hand for the rifle. "This man is our guest."

"No, Ma." He shook his head vigorously. "He's the enemy."

Ma grasped the rifle barrel and raised it upward. "Suppose your father is lost somewhere, and he's found shelter in a young boy's barn. Would you want that boy to shoot him because he's the enemy?"

Jimmy lowered his eyes, the picture of his father roaming the German countryside too vivid to even think about.

Ma cupped his chin in her hand, raising his gaze to hers. "Besides, it's Christmas. Is there any better way to honor God's gift to us than to spare this man?"

"I just want Pa to come home," Jimmy said, his voice little more than a whisper. He let the rifle slide to his side.

"I'm sure that's all Mr. Richter's son wants too." She enveloped Jimmy into a hug, and he buried his face against her shoulder. As she held him tight, the stone of anger and hatred slowly dissolved. When he pulled away, Ma searched his face, and her sweet smile lit up her eyes. "What do you say we go ahead and cut into that chocolate cake I was saving for Christmas dinner? Would you like that?"

Afraid to trust his voice, Jimmy nodded.

"Good." She took the rifle in one hand and placed her other arm around his shoulders as she turned to the German. "You're welcome to join us, Mr. Richter. We have fresh milk too."

"*Nein.* I don't wish to intrude," the German said, but at that moment, his stomach growled loudly.

Laughter bubbled up and out of Jimmy before he could stop it.

"Perhaps one small piece." Mr. Richter held up his finger and thumb to indicate the size. He nodded to Jimmy. "If Herr Fuller does not mind."

Jimmy gazed at the German as if seeing him for the first time. With his bleary eyes and beaten face, the man looked as worn out as a hard-ridden horse that had been put up wet. Not mean. Not dangerous. Just an ordinary man. A man like Pa.

* * *

On Christmas morning, Jimmy woke with a start, surprised he'd slept so late. But then they'd stayed up till after midnight eating chocolate cake and listening to Mr. Richter talk about his homeland. They'd told him about their Christmas star tradition, and he'd talked about his family's sledding parties. Ma had given him clothes to change into, and he'd cleaned up pretty decent. For a German.

When he insisted on sleeping in the workshop, she'd also given him a proper pillow and blanket.

Climbing out of bed, Jimmy hurriedly dressed and raced out of the house. The screen door slammed behind him as he headed for the workshop. He flung open the door, but Mr. Richter was gone. The neatly folded blanket and pillow lay on the bench.

Jimmy picked up a wooden object lying on top of the pillow.

"He's gone." Ma's voice sounded behind him.

"He left us this." Jimmy held up a delicate star. "He sure does know how to whittle."

"It's a beautiful gift. Shall we hang it on our tree?"

He nodded and walked with Ma back toward the house. "I sure hope he makes it home."

* * *

Christmas Eve, 1954
Jim Fuller dangled a finely carved wooden star in front of his seven-month-old son. "And that's the story of our Christmas star," he said as the infant reached up chubby hands to grasp it. "And the reason we wait to put it on our tree until Christmas Eve."

"Another Fuller tradition," said his wife. "It's almost nine o'clock. Shall we go outside?"

Jim handed her the baby and hung the star beside a whittled snowflake near the top of the tree. "I'm ready," he said. "When Ma and Pa come over for dinner tomorrow, I want to be able to tell them we were outside the same time they were."

A few minutes later, he and Polly were staring up at the night sky, pointing out the brightest star in the heavens to their boy.

* * *

An ocean away, though it was the wee hours of the morning, Kurt Richter woke his family and led them outside to search for the Christmas star. He never talked about the war, never mentioned the long stretch he'd endured in a different POW camp before repatriation. Those days were a distant memory he hid deep in his soul.

But as his son pointed to the brightest star in the sky, Kurt remembered another Christmas Eve. He breathed a silent prayer for the Florida boy who had spared his life beneath the Christmas star.

CALLING GRANDMA JEAN

Pam Hanson & Barbara Andrews

"This is the first white Christmas I can remember in a long time," Ellen Stafford said as she looked out the front window. A carpet of white covered the ground, and swirls of snow danced a languid ballet in the fading afternoon light.

Her family had retired to her cozy living room following a bountiful Christmas dinner, and the generous portions of turkey and stuffing, along with the warmth of a crackling fire, made everyone a little drowsy. Hushed carols played on the radio, and the lights on the tree twinkled in the gathering dusk, their colors adding a warm glow to the room.

"It seems like when we were kids, we always had white Christmases," Ellen's son Rick said.

"We always did too," Ellen agreed.

"What was Christmas like when you were little, Grandma?" Ellen's granddaughter Rachel asked. The seven-year-old had abandoned her new doll and wandered over to perch on the arm of Ellen's chair. Ellen liked to reminisce about the central Michigan farm where she'd grown up with her parents and older brother and sister, and she had shared many stories with Rachel about her childhood.

Ellen glanced around the room at her family, from her elderly mother Nancy to Rick and Ann's new baby. She felt so blessed to have four generations gathered round her this Christmas, though she felt a pang of longing for her husband Ted. It was her first Christmas without him.

"I think Rachel has probably heard all your stories by now, Mom," Rick teased.

Ellen laughed, and then hesitated. "Well, I do have one story none of you has heard, not even you, Rick," she said in a wistful voice. "In fact, I've kept it a secret for more than fifty years. I'm not at all sure you will believe it really happened."

Ellen glanced at her mother, Nancy, who had recently celebrated her ninetieth birthday. Nancy had drifted off again in the old red wingback chair that she'd given Ellen when she moved to her apartment in the assisted-living facility. Satisfied that her mother wasn't listening, Ellen thought perhaps it was time to tell the story of what had happened to her so many years ago. She'd treasured it in her heart for such a long time, it was hard to be sure it had really happened.

"I'd love to hear your story, but I'm about to fall asleep," Ann said. "I think I'll put the baby in his bed and have a little nap, if you don't mind."

Ellen smiled and nodded.

When Rachel's mother and baby brother were gone, the little girl snuggled in beside Ellen, ready for the story, as she had done so many times before. "Is this a true story, Grandma?"

Ellen nodded. "Yes. When I was seven years old, like you are now, my grandma Jean lived with us on the farm, and she always made Christmas special for me. You never knew my grandma Jean, Rachel, but I loved her so much.

"That winter, she had a terrible cold and had to go to the hospital. I couldn't bear the idea that Grandma might miss Christmas. I missed her so much, I didn't even go with Dad and my brother and sister when they went to cut down the Christmas tree from our woods."

"That's Great-Uncle Tom and Great-Aunt Judy," Rick explained to Rachel. "You met them last summer."

"Yes. They were older than I was, and they didn't seem to miss Grandma Jean nearly as much as I did. I remember I didn't feel like helping Judy decorate Christmas cookies that year. And when Tom snuck into the parlor to shake packages under the tree and guess what our presents were, I didn't even care what I was getting."

"What *did* you want for Christmas?" Rachel asked.

"I probably wanted a Barbie doll that year," Ellen told her, "but that's not what this story is about." Ellen glanced at her sleeping mother and continued her tale. "Every chance I got, I went up to my little bedroom tucked away under the eaves to ask God to help Grandma Jean get well. The upstairs rooms in our old farmhouse got very cold in the winter, but I'd close the door and get down on my knees on the braided rug Grandma Jean had made for me. I prayed as hard as I could because I knew how sad my grandmother would be if she couldn't come home for Christmas."

"Did God answer your prayers?" Rachel asked in a hushed voice.

"I was sure He would," Ellen told her, "but He seemed to be taking an awfully long time. I didn't know what a hospital was like, but my friend Jessie, who sat by me on the school bus, said it was an awful place. Her grandmother went there and never came home. So naturally, I was scared for Grandma Jean."

Ellen glanced affectionately at her mother and went on. "My mother knew how upset and worried I was about Grandma Jean, so she said we could call the hospital on the telephone to see how she was doing. In those days we had a party line."

"That means that more than one family shared the same phone line," Rick explained for Rachel's benefit. "Sometimes you had to wait until someone else stopped talking before you could use it."

Rachel turned and gave her father an incredulous look.

"Yes, it's true," Ellen assured her. "But that wasn't the problem that day. The phone line must have been down in the storm, because Mom couldn't get a dial tone. Our phone was dead, and I was terribly disappointed not to be able to call the hospital. Grandma didn't have a phone in her room, but a nurse would have been able to tell us how she was doing—but we couldn't get through.

"My parents seemed to be more worried about getting to church that night for Christmas Eve. At least, I thought so at the time. They probably didn't want to alarm me any more, especially when they explained Grandma Jean was much too sick to come home for Christmas.

"Dad was concerned about the snow drifting across the long driveway to the road, so he had to go out and plow, even though he always put tire chains on our big Oldsmobile station wagon so it would get through the snow. My brother Tom was worried about the sheep he was raising to show at the 4-H fair, so Mom went out to the barn with him to check on them. She told Judy to keep an eye on me, but I'm afraid my big sister was more interested in listening to Beach Boys records in her room. That's when I had an idea."

"Uh-oh," Rick said in a teasing tone. "Grandma Ellen's ideas can be big trouble."

Ellen gave him a look of motherly reproof and thought back to the genuine anxiety she'd felt for her beloved grandmother. Even after all these years, she vividly remembered her fear. She hadn't been satisfied with her parents' veiled explanation of Grandma Jean's illness, and she still wished they'd been more forthcoming. Sometimes, she thought now as she looked back, it was better to know the truth, especially for a child of seven with an overactive imagination. She'd been afraid Grandma Jean would die and never come home.

"What was wrong with your grandma?" Rachel asked.

"I believe she had pneumonia," Ellen said. "That's a sickness that can make it hard to breathe."

"So did she come home for Christmas?" Rachel asked, snuggling against Ellen.

"Go on, Mom," Rick encouraged her.

"Well, as I said, I was worried that Grandma Jean would never come home. But somehow, after I prayed as hard as I could," Ellen said, "I knew God wouldn't take her away from me. But I was seven, just like you, Rachel. I needed reassurance."

Ellen looked into the faces of her son and granddaughter, hoping she could convey the faith she'd had that God could work miracles, especially at Christmastime.

"Judy was sixteen then and she wanted to fuss with her hair—the girls wore it in big beehive hairdos, and Judy was always adding hairspray so it would stay in place." Ellen winked. "I think there was a boy she liked who would be at the Christmas Eve service later on. She put out a coloring book for me and told me to stay at the kitchen table until Mom and Dad came back inside. But I had other ideas, and when Judy went back to her room, I forgot all about coloring."

"Were you being naughty?" Rachel asked, wiggling into a more comfortable position.

"I guess you could say that, but I told myself it was Judy's fault for not watching me. I went to the hallway by the front door where our phone was kept in a niche built into the wall. It was a heavy black one you had to dial, not like today's where you punch the numbers," she explained to Rachel. "I wasn't allowed to use the phone on my own. In fact, I hardly ever talked on it. My dad said it was hard enough sharing with other families. He couldn't have his children tying up the line too.

"I sat on the steps—where Mom always sat when she used the phone—and silently said a prayer that Grandma would get well and come home for Christmas. I sat there for what seemed like a long time, listening to Judy's music floating down the stairwell and praying that the phone would start working again."

"And did it?" Rachel asked.

"I'm sure Grandma Ellen will tell us if we're patient," Rick told her.

"I could still hear Judy's music from the stairway. I didn't want to get in trouble, but I just had to call Grandma. So I climbed up on the stool and picked up the receiver, hoping and praying the phone was working again. I wasn't supposed to call anyone without permission, but no one had ever said I couldn't listen for a dial tone."

Rick laughed. "That kind of thinking got me in trouble a few times."

"I remember," Ellen said to her son before continuing. "So I lifted up the receiver and heard nothing. The phone was still dead."

"Did you get in trouble for touching the phone?" Rachel asked, squirming on her lap.

"Rachel, *shh*. Let Grandma tell her story," her father gently chided her. "Go on, Mom."

"I can tell you my parents weren't very happy with me," Ellen said with a smile. "But the important part is coming. I knew there should be a dial tone, but the phone was still silent. Pretty soon my parents would come inside, and we'd have dinner. Then it would be time to leave for church. When we got home, Mom would probably say it was too late to call.

"Mom had taught me that if we ever had an emergency, I should dial zero and talk to the operator. Well, in my mind, this was an emergency. Grandma Jean was all alone in the hospital, and it was Christmas! I had to tell her everything would be all right because I'd been praying for her. I stuck my finger in the hole by the O and slowly moved the dial. Suddenly, I heard a woman's voice speaking. I was so startled I dropped the phone and almost fell off the footstool."

"Who was it?" Rachel asked, her eyes wide.

"I can only say it was a woman's voice, and I remember that it sounded very far away. I thought I must have reached an angel up in heaven. I picked up the receiver again and said, 'Are you still there?' And she was. I told her I *had* to talk to my grandma, and she said, 'I'll put you through now.'

"I waited for a moment, and then suddenly I heard a ringing sound and Grandma said, 'Hello?' I was so happy, I started crying. I said, 'Grandma, it's me!'"

"But wait a minute, Mom. You said there was no dial tone. The line was dead. How could you reach the operator?" Rick asked. And then he added, "And how did she know who your grandma was?"

"I don't know." Ellen shrugged. "It never occurred to me to say her name. The woman never said she was the operator. All I know is, there I was, talking to my beloved grandmother.

"'Oh, don't cry, sweetheart,' Grandma Jean told me. 'Everything is going to be just fine.'"

Ellen paused, anticipating a comment, but Rick only said, "And then what happened?"

"I told her, 'I miss you so much, Grandma! I prayed and prayed God would let you come home for Christmas,'" Ellen said. Even now, after all the years that had passed, tears welled up in her eyes as she remembered.

"Grandma Jean told me, 'Guess what, sweetheart. I *am* coming home for Christmas! I'll get to see you open your presents tomorrow.' She told me to have Dad or Mom call her right back. She told me how much she loved me, and we said good-bye. I hung up the phone. Just then, Mom came into the hallway from outside. I remember that her cheeks were bright red from the cold, and she asked me what I was doing."

"Did you tell her you talked to Grandma Jean?" Rachel asked.

"Oh yes," Ellen said with a wistful smile. "Mom only gave me a funny look and told me to climb down off the footstool. When I explained that Grandma hadn't called, but a lady had gotten her for me, I knew by my mother's expression I was in trouble. But I was so happy about Grandma coming home, it didn't matter. I tried to convince Mom to call the hospital and hear for herself, but when she picked up the phone and held it to her ear, it was still dead."

"You must have missed your grandmother so much, you imagined the conversation," Rick said sympathetically. "You couldn't possibly have spoken to her on a dead phone." He thought for a moment. "Besides, you said your grandma didn't have a phone in her room. You would only have been connected to a nursing station."

"Oh, I know. My parents reminded me of all that and more, but I knew I'd talked with her. I kept insisting they call Grandma and learn for themselves she was ready to come home. My mother was quite cross at first, insisting I'd made up the story. Dad said that no matter how much I wanted something to happen, it wasn't good to tell tales. In the end, Judy was in more trouble than I was because she hadn't taken responsibility for watching me while they were outside. Mom made me promise not to touch the phone again without permission and made me sit on the footstool in the parlor until dinner was ready.

"I cried and cried because Grandma Jean was waiting in the hospital for Dad to drive her home, and no one would believe me. We even had my favorite macaroni and cheese for dinner, but I could hardly swallow a bite. Mom felt my forehead and had me lie down on the couch, and she put a cold cloth on my red eyes until I changed clothes for church. Grandma had made me a new dress to wear Christmas Eve. I remember that it was a green-and-red plaid, and she'd knitted a red sweater to wear over it, special just for me. But that night it didn't make me feel special. I just felt miserable because no one believed me."

"So did your grandma come home for Christmas?" Rachel asked, looking anxiously up into Ellen's face.

"You'll see," Ellen said. "The church was filling up when we got there, our fingers and toes cold because the heater in the station wagon didn't work very well. Mom let us walk to the front where a Nativity scene was set up under the Christmas tree. Usually I loved the little figures of Mary, Joseph, and baby Jesus. The wise men wore sparkly hats, and the shepherds had wooly miniature sheep. That night, though, I barely even saw them through my tears. My parents didn't believe me. Grandma Jean wanted to come home, and I couldn't convince my parents to go get her.

"The service seemed to take forever. I prayed to baby Jesus, hoping He could bring my grandmother home for His birthday, but my heart wasn't in it. God had already made Grandma Jean well, but my parents didn't believe me.

"Dad was hustling us into the station wagon, fretting over the heavy snow that would be filling our driveway again, when Mr. Barnes, a man from the congregation, stopped his car right behind us. I stood and watched him instead of climbing into the backseat, but Mom was too distracted to notice.

"'Glad I caught you,' he said to my dad, stepping out of his car into the glow of his headlights. I remember seeing his breath puff out with every word. 'Your mother was trying to call you all afternoon, but I guess your phone is out. She knew I'd see you at the Christmas Eve service, so she asked me to give you a message.'

"Dad was silent for a long moment, then asked in a hoarse voice, 'My mother called you?'"

"Mom," Rick started to interrupt, but Ellen silenced him by shaking her head.

"'Yes,' Mr. Barnes went on. 'She couldn't reach you. Sorry to hear she's been sick, but there's good news. The doctor said she can come home anytime. She wants you to come get her tomorrow morning because the roads are pretty bad tonight.' He pushed his coat sleeve up to glance at his watch. 'Anyway, the hospital doesn't check people out this late.'"

"So she really had been calling?" Rick asked skeptically.

Ellen nodded. "Believe me, my heart was pounding with excitement. I wanted to remind my parents I'd told the truth about talking to my grandmother, but they were frowning instead of celebrating. Dad wanted to know what time she'd called Mr. Barnes, and he said around suppertime. Mom wanted to know whether she'd mentioned talking to me, but she hadn't."

"Did your grandma come home for Christmas?" Rachel asked again.

"Let Grandma finish the story," Rick told her.

"Mom and Dad didn't say a word on the way home except to scold Judy when she asked whether she had to go to the hospital with them. We all got into pajamas and robes and had a Christmas Eve treat, but all I wanted to do was talk about Grandma Jean coming home.

"Mom always made a special dessert for us to eat after the Christmas Eve service, keeping it a secret until the time to enjoy it. That night, I remember it was chocolate pie with whipped cream topping, my favorite, but I could barely eat. Not even the taste of chocolate could make me forget the wonderful news Mr. Barnes had told us. And I couldn't understand why Mom and Dad weren't saying anything about it or about my call to Grandma.

"When Dad said we had to bring Grandma home before we opened presents Christmas morning, I couldn't have been happier. He said she'd want to watch us open our gifts. I insisted on going, even though my mom, brother, and sister were staying home. Grandma had talked to me on the phone, and now she'd tell my parents. Then they would know I was telling the truth.

"The next morning I woke up before it was even light outside. I was so excited to go get Grandma Jean. After we ate breakfast, my dad and I piled into our big old station wagon, and Mom, Judy, and Tom remained at home.

"We drove for some time before my dad finally spoke. 'Mr. Barnes told me your grandmother did try to contact us,' he said in a solemn voice, his eyes never leaving the road. I held my breath, waiting for him to admit I'd talked to her. Instead he asked if I knew the phone wasn't working. Then he said, 'Honey, I don't think you're fibbing, okay? I don't understand it, exactly, but I believe you. But I think this is very upsetting to your mother. She thinks you're telling stories, sweetheart. So will you promise me something?'

"That was when he asked me never to mention it to my mother again." Ellen glanced over at her sleeping parent.

"The important thing, he said, was that God had answered our prayers. Grandma Jean wasn't sick anymore, and she could be with us for Christmas. Then he asked me again to promise not to talk about my phone call again. I didn't want to upset my mom. And I didn't want her to think I was making up stories that weren't true. So I never mentioned it to her again.

"I remember the roads were pretty clear that morning because the snow had stopped. Once we reached the county hospital, we didn't keep Grandma Jean waiting very long. I couldn't wait to see her. When we got inside, I saw it wasn't such a scary place at all. Grandma Jean was dressed and waiting in a sunny room with crisp white curtains.

"'I'm so glad you got my message,' she told Dad, and then she winked at me, as if we were sharing some big secret, and gave me a hug. I opened my mouth to say something, but Dad shook his head, and I knew he didn't want me to mention the mysterious phone call to anyone, not even Grandma."

When Ellen finished her story, she looked at her son and his daughter, not knowing what reaction to expect.

"Did you really talk to your grandma Jean?" Rachel asked.

Ellen sighed. "You know, I have asked myself that same question many times over the years. But I really believe I did." She paused. "I know God answered my prayers. Later on, I found out just how sick my grandmother actually was. My parents weren't sure she would live."

"But you promised not to tell," Rachel said, sounding distressed. She glanced over at Grandma Nancy, whose eyes were still closed.

"I know my father would understand after all this time," Ellen said thoughtfully. "He knew I was telling the truth, and I think it's okay that I pass the story on to you now."

"I believe you, Grandma Ellen," Rachel said, reaching up to put her arms around her neck.

"I think I do too," Rick said thoughtfully.

Ellen glanced over at her mother. Nancy's eyes opened, and mother and daughter looked at each other for a long moment. Nancy nodded, almost imperceptibly. She'd been listening all along.

Ellen's heart swelled. *Mom knows.*

"Ellen, I'm glad you finally told that story," the elderly woman said quietly. "Honestly, I always wondered why you never brought it up again. When it happened, I just couldn't believe it. I did think you were making up a story. But your dad knew, somehow, and much later, he told me." She sighed. "I was wrong, dear, and I'm glad I lived to admit the truth to my daughter. I'm sorry."

Tears welled in Ellen's eyes. Her lingering doubts had been put to rest. With the faith of a child, she realized, all things truly are possible. And maybe one day, she thought, Rachel would tell her own granddaughter the story of how God answered a little girl's Christmas prayers.

The Christmas Thief

Ashley Clark

Fading sunlight cast a glow through the colored mosaics of the old Charleston church onto the cobblestone beneath. From the wrong side of the church walls, Samuel Thompson hummed along with the carols. Snowflakes fell in a lazy swirl as Sam huddled under his worn sweatshirt and leaned against an old street lamp in the downtown square. All around him, people looked up in awe of the snow Charleston seldom saw, as if it were some kind of gift on this Christmas Eve.

The congregation inside the church was finishing their song when a car stopped at the red light and honked at Sam. A man waved a five-dollar bill through the rolled-down window, even as two cars pulled to a stop behind him. Sam hurried along the street to take the money before the light turned green. He jogged back to his place on the sidewalk and looked through the windows of the church once more. It wasn't long ago that he'd been on the other side of the church walls.

He shoved the bill into his pocket. At least it was enough to buy a small meal tonight. Last week, someone had given him a twenty, and he'd splurged on a bus ride to the Festival of Lights. For a few hours as he rode through the streets lined with colorful, twinkling lights, he'd felt normal again. But then he'd come back to his bench outside the church, and reality had dimmed the small flickering of hope. He shouldn't have spent his money so foolishly. The next day, he'd grown so hungry he'd resorted to taking pears and apples from the Christmas basket wreaths on display on porches.

Sam puffed into his dirt-smudged hands to gather what little warmth he could muster and shifted his body to get a better view of the congregation coming out from the doors of the church.

He never thought he'd end up like this, forty-two and homeless. Never thought he'd be hoping for a handout on Christmas Eve. This isn't how his life was supposed to go.

The grand doors opened, and men and women passed Sam one by one, dressed in their Christmas Eve best just as he had been for so many years. He could almost hear their thoughts as they passed—*Alcoholic. Lazy. Godless man*—none of which were true.

In his mind, he was still Sam Thompson, aspiring archeologist. Someday husband. Someday father. Someday…when he got back on his feet.

He'd never planned to lose his very specialized job, and then his picket-fence home, and then find that part-time work wasn't enough to make ends meet. Before long, his dreams had become the next casualty.

A gust of winter wind gripped Sam with deep cold. He closed his eyes and tried to remember the feeling of the warm Florida sand between his toes and the taste of now-extravagant sweet tea.

For a moment he remembered, and his heart ached. Then his eyes fluttered open as someone coming out from the church tripped over the frayed backpack at his feet.

Sam couldn't believe his eyes.

Evelyn Rose.

Sam dropped to one knee and pretended to tie his worn shoelaces. Maybe she'd assume he'd just stopped to tie them and that he didn't actually live on the street. But then he watched as Evelyn's ever-knowing gaze traveled to the backpack beside him, and his heart fell as he realized how filthy he must seem.

The last time he'd seen Evelyn, he'd worn Dockers, a trimmed beard, and his favorite red polo. He'd told her in his usually confident way that he'd always love her, but he'd been offered an internship with a world-renowned archeologist and he simply couldn't pass up the opportunity.

Funny how life turns things upside down. Years ago, Sam practically left Evelyn at the altar for a career that later left him on the street. Today, Sam's beard was anything but neatly trimmed, his dark hair needed washing, and he was pretty sure he'd sold that polo at a yard sale, trying to get more rent money. But Evelyn still had the glow of an angel.

"Sam, are you... are you..."

Homeless.

She couldn't seem to say the word. But maybe she didn't need to.

A wedding ring caught glimmers of lamplight in the fading sun, scattering what little hope Sam still held across the cobblestone street. It wasn't as if Evelyn would be interested in sharing his life any longer...not this life, anyway.

No, Samuel Thompson had become a failure, through and through.

Evelyn leaned closer and squinted as her sight adjusted from the light of the church to the twilight depths of the evening. "Sam?"

It took all he could muster to meet her gaze as little tears slipped down her gentle face. "Evelyn."

She did something he hadn't expected then. She sat down beside him. She was silent for a few moments, her eyes doing all the talking.

Finally, she whispered the words that were thick in the air. "What happened to you?"

Sam shrank under the weight of the question and scraped dirt from underneath his fingernails as he struggled to think of a proper reply.

She took his hand, and his skin trembled at the contact. How long had it been since someone had offered a hand? How long had it been since he'd felt like a worthy human being?

When they'd last met, all the success of the world had been upon his horizon.

Or so it had seemed.

"I failed, Ev. The floor fell out from under me. Not long after I landed my dream job, things took a turn for the worse in the economy. As the newest staff member, I took the first round of pay cuts. Not long after, I was the first one laid off. Meanwhile, I just couldn't let go of the life I was accustomed to having. That ridiculous car, the house…my art collection. I lost everything. Hard as I fought to keep it, I couldn't keep up. And without a place of residence, well, who would want to hire me? I had no one to turn to, and I didn't want the family members who could have helped to know how desperate I had become."

Evelyn leaned in closer and stroked his hand gently. "And your hope?"

"My hope?"

"It's what drew me to you in the first place and ultimately what took you away." She caught his gaze and held it, refusing to let him go with a blink. "Your hope is gone, Sam. I can see it in your eyes."

With all that Sam had lost, hope was the last thing on his list of worries. Yet there was a striking truth in Evelyn's words. She always had been able to cut through to the heart of things. If only he could visit his younger self and explain that a woman like Evelyn was so rare and so valuable, she was worth giving up everything for, even his selfish dreams.

If he'd married her, there was no telling where he might be today. They might have been sharing a Christmas meal tonight in a charming home along the Charleston waterfront. They might have been happy.

No, they *would* have been happy. He was sure of it.

Instead, his own ambitions had gotten in the way of this beautiful gift God had put in his pathway.

Sam's warm breath turned to fog in the cold winter air. "Evelyn, I'm sorry. I am so, so sorry."

"Sam, no." She shook her head. "It was for the best. I was practically a child when we were dating, and I was jealous of your work. I understand now that you needed to take that internship. Really."

"Still, I'd feel better if you forgave me for my selfish choices. I really did care about you, Ev."

She smiled. "I know, Sam." She pulled him into a hug, and he grimaced to think of how he must smell after days of not showering. Then she pulled back and looked in his eyes as if she'd suddenly gotten an idea. "Stay here."

A few minutes later, she returned with a large bowl of chicken and dumplings from the corner restaurant, his favorite.

Sam forced himself to eat at a normal pace. How long had it been since he had eaten a fresh, full meal like this rather than someone's cold leftovers or the cheap peanut butter and jelly sandwiches he splurged on anytime he got some money?

Evelyn watched him eat. As he finished, she pressed a crisp bill into his palm.

"No, Ev. I can't." This was all so humbling that Sam wanted to cry. Everything had gone wrong. His swallow was painful. He didn't even need to look at the bill to know it was too much. "I can't accept this."

Evelyn gently closed his fingers around the bill. "If you really want to make it up to me, there is something you can do."

"What's that?" His heart jumped with the possibility of closure with Evelyn, even if it wasn't in the way he'd always hoped it would be.

She nodded toward the church. "I want you to go inside and find your hope again."

Sam bit his lower lip. He shivered as the wind whipped mercilessly through the holes of his jeans. If nothing else, perhaps he could appease Evelyn and find a reprieve from the winter weather.

Evelyn stood and reached out her hand, helping him to stand. "Come on, Sam. Sometimes second chances must be sought rather than given. And it *is* Christmas Eve. Shouldn't you be in church?"

Sam laughed, the sound rough and hearty to his own ears. He couldn't remember laughing in months. "You drive a hard bargain, but I'll see what I can do."

She looked straight into his eyes. "Sam, it really was good seeing you. I know God hasn't given up His work in your life."

He forced a smile to his lips. God hadn't forgotten about him? Well, He certainly had a strange way of showing it.

Rather than say as much to Evelyn, Sam gave her a grateful good-bye, then slung his backpack over his shoulder and made his way up the church steps.

Sam pulled open the thick wooden door and breathed in deep. The smell of dripping beeswax candles, salvation, and Christmas trees was thick in the air of the old sanctuary.

He remembered a time when the smell of the sanctuary had been ordinary. A time when he had felt he belonged in a place like this, before the realities of failure and hopelessness had trapped him on the street. A time before a park bench became his bed at night, the chatter of passersby his only company.

No. God no longer had any use for his life. Sam had mangled it up too badly.

Bright poinsettias and pure white Christmas lilies lined the aisles of the church, now empty except for the footprints and prayers the congregation had left behind.

Sam made his way down the aisle and took a seat in the third row. His old pew from years ago felt at once familiar and forsaken. Guilt washed over his bones as he realized the dynamics of the choices he had made.

He never should have broken up with Evelyn three months before their wedding day. He never should have stopped looking for a job. And most of all, he never should've given up his faith in the God who redeems.

But he had. He had done all of those things, and now he was worse than helpless. He was alone.

"God," Sam whispered into the holy air of the large sanctuary, "why did You forget about me?" He grasped the back of the pew in front of him, and his eyes stung with tears. "Is there any hope left for me, when I've messed things up so terribly?"

Sam waited for a response. Nothing happened.

Evelyn had said if he sought hope, he would find it, and he'd known that to be true at one point in his life. It was fine thinking for a woman like Evelyn, a woman with all the opportunities in the world, who had made good choices with her life. But was there a point when a person made enough wrong choices that hope, very simply, could not be found?

Sam rubbed his palms against the worn denim of his jeans. He felt like weeping, but his soul had grown too calloused to open with a flood of mourning. His gaze darted around the sanctuary, drinking in the biblical scenes on the stained-glass windows as the passing twilight turned to night on this Christmas Eve.

Then he saw the antique Geneva Bible openly displayed. The same Bible his mother had admired when he was a child. The Bible that had sparked his interest in archeology.

Sam's mother had explained to him that the Bible's origin went back long into history and that it was very valuable. Sam had been so fascinated by the artifact as a child that he'd dug holes all through their backyard, hoping to find his own artifacts.

That Bible had changed his life. It had given him a dream to follow. And now, maybe it could help him once more to find his hope.

He needed a closer look. Could the Bible spark a new dream, or at least bring the comfort of memories with his mother?

Then Sam got an idea.

The Bible was easily worth enough to buy a used car to sleep in. Maybe then he could drive to a decent job and make enough money to get back on his feet. At the very least, it would buy him some hot meals.

But he'd never resorted to stealing before, as bad as things had been, aside from the fruit on the basket wreaths.

He couldn't steal the Bible...could he? Was this really what had become of his life?

Hands trembling and stomach churning, Sam moved down the aisle.

I have no other options left. Maybe this is the way to find the hope Evelyn was talking about.

The Bible lay open on the podium where the pastor had just used it to preach. Sam remembered the pastor always used this Bible during his sermons. He used to say the text was not an artifact, but the living, breathing Word of God, available to all, and he refused to keep it locked up.

Before he could think better of it and talk himself out of what must be done, Sam reached forward, grabbed the Geneva

Bible, and tucked it inside his hooded sweatshirt, careful not to bend any of the pages. He may be a thief, but he was still a historian, and he wouldn't damage a beautiful artifact.

As Sam's gaze traveled upward to the wooden, gabled ceiling, he thought he heard footsteps behind him. Someone cleared his throat.

Slowly, Sam turned.

Pastor Clune. The same man who had pastored the church when Sam and his mother had attended years ago. Before she grew ill. Before Sam grew ashamed.

Pastor Clune looked the same as he always had. Round glasses, a thin frame, and a kind countenance. His hair had fully grayed in the years Sam had been gone.

Sam closed his eyes. He should have looked more carefully around the sanctuary.

He waited for the minister to speak. Pastor Clune had every right to call 9-1-1. Sam could only imagine how much harder it would be to get a job with a criminal record.

Sam reached into his old sweatshirt and pulled out the Bible. Pastor Clune held out his hand. Did he recognize Sam? He didn't seem to.

Sam summoned the courage to meet the minister's gaze. He knew what he would find there. Disgust, judgment, pity.

But instead, he found a look of gentleness and love.

Sam handed Pastor Clune the Bible he'd just attempted to steal.

"Are you...are you going to press charges?" His voice sounded raspy and raw even to his own ears. Sam braced himself for the possibility of a Christmas meal served in a jail cell. After all, wasn't that where he belonged? Besides, jail might not be so bad—he'd at least have three good meals a day and shelter.

Pastor Clune held a fist to his mouth in silence as he considered his options. Then, deliberately, he spoke. "I say we keep this incident between the two of us. But only on one condition."

Sam sighed. His shame could only be trumped by his relief. Pastor Clune's mercy was nothing short of a Christmas miracle. "I'll do anything you ask."

The pastor returned the Bible to its rightful place on the podium. The Bible sat open once again to all who passed through the sanctuary.

Then he stepped forward and clapped a hand on Sam's shoulder. "Come with me."

"Where are we going?"

Pastor Clune smiled. "To my house."

Sam frowned. "Your house? But why?"

"Well, I figure from the looks of things, you haven't had a home-cooked meal in a while. And I tell you what—if you agree to listen to the story of that Bible, I'll give it to you. Deal?" He walked back up the steps to the podium and took hold of the book.

Sam was taken aback. Didn't this man know he was a thief? Hearing the history of the Bible from Pastor Clune seemed a small penance for what he'd just tried to do.

Sam shook his head. "Sir, I don't understand. What have I done to deserve this kindness?"

The pastor began to walk down the church aisle and opened the door that led to his parsonage across the courtyard. Sam followed him.

"Have you ever heard the story of the prodigal son?" Pastor Clune asked.

Sam moistened his lips, tasting dirt. "It's been a long time."

Pastor Clune stopped near an iron garden bench. "Well, the important thing is, the prodigal son comes home." He held up the Bible. "Now let me tell you the story of how this Bible I'm holding changes lives." He shook his head and grinned. "But I have to tell you, it's a dangerous story. If you aren't looking for a change in your life... well, it's best to leave now. Because this story has a history of giving hope."

Sam doubted the story could be that powerful for a man as broken as himself. But what did he have to lose?

He looked at the lamplight on the cobblestone streets and didn't feel as cold with the promise of the home-cooked meal to come. "I'm all ears."

Pastor Clune set the Bible on the bench and bent down to pull a couple stray weeds from the winter flowers near the sidewalk. "So, there was this man named Isaac Cooper, a man of great learning who made many unfortunate choices in his life."

Unfortunate choices? Sam's interest piqued.

"Having burned all his bridges, so to speak, Isaac knew it was time for a major change, so he decided to come to America."

Sam hugged his arms around his chest as snow flurries began to fall. "But the Bible... it's a Geneva text. My mother told me its history runs back as far as the United States."

Had his mother been wrong? Somehow the value of the text seemed a bit diminished if it were not actually an early-American artifact, but rather something this Isaac fellow had more recently brought into the country.

The minister turned from his work in the garden and stood. "Your mother was correct. You see, Isaac Cooper was a Pilgrim."

"A Pilgrim?"

Pastor Clune might have lit up the whole courtyard with his smile. He rubbed the dirt off his hands and put one on Sam's shoulder. "Come now, it's getting cold out. Let's get inside, and I'll tell you the rest of the story."

Sam's mind raced as he tried to make sense of Pastor Clune's words. Within minutes, he found himself among the bustling hum of the minister's family as they finished preparations for the sumptuous meal.

A Christmas tree trimmed with handmade ornaments and colorful lights took center stage in the main room adjacent to the open kitchen, and the minister's family gathered around the piano, singing Christmas carols, as Mrs. Clune busied herself getting the table ready.

Sam's stomach groaned with hunger so strong he thought he might be sick. The earlier chicken and dumplings weren't doing much in the way of satisfying his appetite. How long had it been since he'd smelled freshly made bread, whipped potatoes, and baked turkey? Might as well have been another lifetime.

Pastor Clune nudged Sam with his elbow. "Go ahead and try a bite. My lovely wife is the best cook in the city. She's always sayin' she's going to try out for one of those Food Network shows, but I'd have to follow her there, because I tell you, without her cooking, I don't know how I'd survive."

Mrs. Clune swatted the air at his praise, her plump cheeks blushing. She opened the refrigerator and reached for a pitcher, then poured a glass and handed it to Sam.

"What's this?" he asked. The warmth he saw in her smile felt as unfamiliar as the coolness of the glass in his callused fingertips.

"Sweet tea." Mrs. Clune said the words as if they should already be known. Then she stopped halfway to the oven and spun around to face him. "You do *like* sweet tea, don't you?"

Sam smiled. "This is South Carolina, isn't it?" He took a sip, trying not to seem too eager for a drink. His throat had gone dry from thirsting so long. If only Mrs. Clune knew that an hour ago, Sam had steadied the longing of his parched throat by closing his eyes and thinking of a tall glass of tea like the one he now held.

She laughed and wagged her finger at him. "Now that's what I like to hear. Soon as I finish fixing our meal, I'll get some sheets for the sofa."

Sam's brow creased. "Sheets?"

Mrs. Clune put one hand on her hip. "For you to sleep on tonight." She wagged the finger at him again. "No guest of ours is sleeping out on the street."

He shouldn't accept their offer to stay. But desperation had a way of knocking humility into a person, and Sam knew if he declined, he wouldn't have any other offers. He dipped his head in a nod of thanks. "Sure appreciate that."

She bit her bottom lip and looked Sam up and down, as if she were taking some kind of measurements. "You're about my husband's height. I'm sure he's got some clothes that'd fit you. When you two are done talking, we'll get you set up with a warm shower and a new pair of jeans."

She turned back to the refrigerator and moved the tea pitcher, clearly satisfied with her generous plans for Sam's evening. "Now, y'all find yourselves something else to do and stop crowding up my kitchen."

Pastor Clune laughed. "I know when to take a hint." He gestured toward a hallway. "Come on, son. Let's head to my study, and I'll tell you the rest of the story."

Sam followed, glass in hand.

A quiet tranquility enveloped them as they stepped into the office. The caroling of the pastor's family and the smell of the feast to come grew muted.

"Have a seat, son."

A black cat with one tuxedo stripe leisurely stepped across the back of the sofa where Sam had planned to sit down.

Pastor Clune noticed his hesitation and laughed. "Don't mind Paul." He gently tucked the cat under his arm and set it on the floor. "We call him that because he always used to sit outside the church, terrorizing the congregation as they came out. Oh, he'd hiss and swat and just carry on. But I kept leaving him food and milk, and sure enough, one day he saw the light. Stepped right into our home and never looked back. So we like to say he went from Saul to Paul."

Sam smiled at the cat. He remembered enough about the apostle's story to appreciate the similarities.

"Say," the minister said, stepping closer. "You'll pardon my old man's memory, but you look awfully familiar. Have we met?" He squinted, trying to make the connection. Then recognition seemed to dawn on him. "Why, you aren't Sarah Thompson's boy? Sam?"

Sam winced at his mother's name. What would she think if she could see him now? So consumed by failure that all he could think about was the comfort of the couch upon which he sat, and the crispness of the tea against his lips...

He took a deep breath, nodding. "Yes, sir. That's me. The one and only."

"I'm so sorry for your loss." He looked down at his hands, wrinkled by age and the experiences it brought. "She was a godly woman."

Maybe it was the warmth of the room or the comfort of its walls. It could have been the smell of a Christmas meal and the memories it brought. But for a reason Sam couldn't quite explain, tears began to fall, and he allowed himself to remember—really remember—his mother for the first time in so long. The stories she would tell, the way her laughter hung in the air, and most of all, her firm belief that with faith, anything was possible.

Looking around the pastor's cozy office, Sam had to wonder if maybe she hadn't been wrong.

Perhaps a little part of him still hoped that he could, after all, make something different of his life. That maybe his homelessness was just one chapter of a larger story, and maybe, like Joseph in a foreign jail, God *was* still with him after all.

Pastor Clune watched with a steady look of empathy in his eyes. Sam had seen so much pity, he'd come to recognize the difference. No, the minister didn't seem to pity Sam at all. Instead, he looked at Sam as if he saw the man Sam used to be and the man he'd hoped to become.

It had been so long since a person had shown Sam kindness, he'd forgotten how it felt to be treated like a human being. But it was best to keep his expectations in check. By tomorrow, he'd be homeless and hungry again...just another man on the streets.

Sam leaned back in his seat and crossed his arms, then wiped stubborn tears from his cheeks.

The pastor pulled a handkerchief from his desk drawer and handed it to Sam. Sam dabbed at his tears, now even more humbled in the presence of this godly man. His eyes stung from the sudden release of emotion he'd held back for so long. He needed to pull himself together. Allowing this kind of emotion to pour forth was only adding salt to a wound that could never heal—at least, it wouldn't heal as long as Sam was living on the side of the cobblestone streets.

Pastor Clune handed his prized Bible to Sam. The cover was worn and fragile, yet somehow, remarkably strong.

"I shouldn't be touching this," Sam said. He looked down at the grime under his fingernails. "It holds such value, and I'm...well...a mess."

But the pastor just shook his head, as the faint sound of the family carolers in the other room changed from "O Come All Ye Faithful" to "Silent Night." The latter song had always been Sam's favorite. His mother used to sing it to him as a child.

Sam looked down at the Bible in his hands, and a shiver slid down his spine. How had he even considered stealing such a precious artifact? "So, you were saying the Bible once belonged to a Pilgrim."

Pastor Clune took the recliner across from Sam and settled in. He folded his hands against his stomach and leaned back, a sparkle in his eyes that showed how close the story was to his heart. "A Pilgrim indeed. Intent on paving a path to fortune in the New World, Isaac set off toward what would become America. He expected to be challenged by the journey. But what he didn't expect was to be challenged by the other Pilgrims."

"Challenged in what way?"

"Well, you see, a funny thing happened while Isaac was off accumulating the riches of the world. He lost his heart in the process. And I tell you, nothing will make you more aware of a lost heart than hardship." Pastor Clune stopped and looked at Sam—straight through him—with a gaze that was piercing and deliberate. Pastor Clune continued. "Isaac grew ill on the ship, and grew tired of the other passengers' insistence he turn to God. After all, why should he turn toward a God who allowed his journey to be so hard?"

Sam looked at the Bible in his hands. He, too, had felt that way about the kindhearted God he'd once known. "What happened next?"

"The other Pilgrims wouldn't let up. Finally, Isaac thought of a compromise. He told them he would read the Bible they kept placing at his bedside if they would leave him alone. Convinced they had the stronger end of the deal, the other Pilgrims agreed. Through the swaying of the ship and by the glimmers of the morning sun, Isaac read that Bible cover to cover. And with nothing left in his life or his future but the cry of recovery and the hope of a new life in the New World, he read it again. He read it so many times that by the time they arrived in America, he'd memorized his favorite passages and knew the stories beginning to end."

Pastor Clune looked down at the Bible in Sam's hands as he spoke. Sam could certainly identify with the emptiness that a life filled with material wealth brought. Even before he'd lost everything he owned, Sam had begun to lose the fire in his soul, and if he were honest with himself, that was really the worst of his losses.

The pastor shifted in his seat, then continued. "When they finally saw land, Isaac fell to his knees aboard the ship. For though he was weak in his body, his soul had grown strong. The passage he had intended to take toward riches had turned into another kind of passage entirely. A passage not across the Pacific, but across the struggles and the doubts and the failures of the human soul. A passage toward hope, toward healing, and redemption, most importantly of all. Isaac fell to his knees that day and committed his life and his heart to God. He survived that first difficult winter and many after, and he always kept the Geneva Bible close by. He often said a story close to the body is a story close to the heart and never left his home without the company of this Bible."

Sam leaned forward on the sofa. And for the first time since he'd arrived, with the old Bible cradled in his hands, Sam actually began to feel as if he belonged.

Pastor Clune rubbed his aged hands and clasped them together as if in prayer. "For that reason, when Isaac was an old man and grew ill many years later, his son wanted to bury him with his Bible, assuming the suggestion would bring his dying father comfort. But Isaac refused. Oh, how he refused. He said this valuable Word must never be locked up and most definitely never buried, for the victory it had given him in life far outweighed any comfort it could offer in death."

Warmth like a fireside burned in Sam's heart, through the walls he'd put up and the fears, the discouragement, and the doubts. It was as if his soul had quite suddenly and quite simply awakened. And he knew he would never be the same, having heard the story of the Bible in his hands. For the story was not only Isaac's. The story was also his own.

The minister smiled the kind of smile he might give a long-lost friend. "Isaac Cooper, you see, was my great-great-great-grandfather's father. And that, son, is the reason we keep this Bible open on the podium, because we believe, just as Isaac did, that the value of the artifact is far surpassed by the value of the story inside."

Sam should have felt guilty then for wanting to steal the Bible. Just a short while ago he certainly had. But in the place of his old guilt and feelings of shame, peace flooded his soul, for now he was a different man. His hands had been washed.

He hadn't said an elaborate prayer or given a large sum. He hadn't walked down an aisle or seen lightning in the clouds. Yet redemption had surely come.

For just as Isaac bowed on the ship, Sam bowed his heart and knew that he, too, had finally struck ground.

This Christmas, he would celebrate the baby born in the manger. But so much more than that, he would celebrate the baby who'd come to save the world, and as part of that world, Sam's own heart. His mother always used to say the good Lord knows when even a sparrow falls, and they matter to Him, every one. Now, Sam finally understood. For he had fallen, and though there were so many sparrows, God had seen him and breathed life back into his wings.

Hope had indeed given him flight.

Sam gently rubbed his finger along the faded cover of the Bible, thankful for the witness of Isaac, and even before that, the other Pilgrims. Thankful that neither time nor age had affected the power of the story inside.

Sam stood from his place on the couch and handed the precious Bible back to Pastor Clune. "You need to keep this Bible," he said. "It's already done its work in my heart."

With a smile, the minister took the book from Sam's outstretched hands. "Watching you as I told the story, I suspected as much." He stood and placed his hand on Sam's shoulder as he led Sam toward the door. "You know, I could use some help around here, if you're interested. Tending to the garden, keeping the sanctuary tidy. Wouldn't pay much, but you could stay in our missionary room until you get back on your feet."

Sam felt like weeping all over again. "Absolutely. It would be an honor."

Pastor Clune patted him a couple times on the shoulder and reached for the door handle. "It's settled then. You'll start day after tomorrow."

"Why the day after?" The smell of a feast greeted Sam full on as he stepped through the doorway and into the hall. Excitement wrapped its arms around his chest as he thought of the meal and the days to come.

"Because tomorrow you will be spending Christmas with us."

Sam grinned then, the first of many smiles to come, for he had entered the church a Christmas thief and left with the greatest gift of all.

POSTCARDS AT CHRISTMAS

Julie Carobini

On this Black Friday morning inside the Holly Hills Charity Thrift Store, the air hung heavy with moisture and heat. Olivia Young, the store's thirty-one-year-old proprietor, peeked at the crowd of shoppers browsing in her aisles and considered it a miracle of sorts. She had always believed in miracles—even though she had yet to witness one for herself—and at the sight before her, Olivia would have to say that perhaps the season ahead held promise.

Christmas music wafted through the store speakers as Olivia spied an unopened box perched on the rickety table at the back of the store. She turned to her assistant, Claire, who was counting out change to a frazzled mom on this first day of Christmas shopping. "Watch the front, okay? I'm going to dig into that donated box over there."

Claire peered at her over her glasses. "Let's hope there's something good inside. It's been so busy this morning that by noon, we may just have to strip those Christmas lights off the wall and sell those too."

Olivia laughed. "Not a bad problem to have." She lifted the box and wandered to the front counter. Peering inside, she frowned.

"What is it?" asked Claire. "Crystal? Silver?"

Olivia's shoulders slumped. She shook her head. "Paper."

"Okay. All right. I can work with that...paper. Hmm. First-year anniversary gift, right?"

Olivia dug deeper into the box. "Wait a sec—Books! Nice ones!" She pulled the dusty copies out of the box. "Oh, and they're classics!"

Olivia began to wipe down and price the beautiful hard-cover books. She had yet to spot many e-readers in her small town, and so it seemed to her that these classics would certainly be snapped up and placed under someone's tree this season.

She brushed her fingers across the textured cover of *The Secret Garden*—one of her favorites. Despite the crowd milling about the shop on this morning after Thanksgiving, her mind wandered to a Yorkshire moor on a dewy morning...

"Did you hear me?" An elderly woman wearing her Sunday best frowned at her.

Olivia blinked. "Sorry?"

"I am ready to pay for my purchases."

"I'd be happy to help you." But as she moved to put the book on the counter, a postcard slipped out. Then another. She picked one up, its photo of the sparkling sea lulling her away from the task at hand. How she longed to see such places.

"Excuse me?"

Olivia snapped from her reverie and dropped the card. "Of course."

For the next fifteen minutes, she rang up a steady stream of shoppers. The townspeople had gone through a lot in recent years, what with factories closing and other job prospects whittling down in this part of northwestern Pennsylvania, so Olivia and her lone employee had hatched an idea to make the neighborhood thrift store as welcoming as the fancier stores in nearby St. Martha's.

By the number of customers who had stepped across the threshold since 7 AM, Olivia would say that their plan had been a success. When they finally reached a lull, she turned to Claire. "Let's get these books displayed before the next flurry, okay?"

"Sure thing."

Olivia fluttered the pages of the book that held the beautiful postcards and several more dropped onto the counter. "What in the world...?"

Eleven of them. Eleven postcards, all sent from breathtaking seaside locales. One was postmarked last week.

Claire picked one up, flipped it over, and adjusted her bifocals. "Belinda Marini." She paused. "Thought I knew everyone in this town, but can't say I've heard of her."

"Me neither." Olivia turned each one over. "They're all addressed to Belinda Marini over on Township Way."

Claire read aloud. "'Happy Christmas, Mother! See you next year! Love, J.'"

"She couldn't have meant for these treasures to be donated."

Claire shrugged. "You know, they would make beautiful additions to that idea board you have going in the office..."

Olivia smirked. "Stop making fun of my *dream* board."

"Not making fun. I had dreams too when I was your age. I just hope you actually follow some of yours while you can. You know, do some traveling, find yourself a handsome man to settle down with."

"Claire! I'm only thirty-one. There's time." Olivia stacked the cards in a neat pile and deftly changed the subject. "Guess I'm paying Belinda Marini a visit later today."

* * *

The house looked still. Except for the lack of light, though, it resembled every other house in the neighborhood. Cement steps framed by black wrought iron rails led to a plain wood-and-glass front door. The white clapboard siding needed a good scrubbing, as did the dusty mailbox nailed to the left of the entry. The sidewalk, however, had been neatly cleared of snow.

Olivia knocked on the door and waited. Nothing. She pushed the rusty button near the mailbox but heard no sound. Her gloved knuckles were poised to knock again when a man's voice interrupted her from behind.

"You're not going to find anyone there."

She spun around, heart battering her chest. In the darkness, she could make out his round shape, but not much else. She steadied herself as her eyes adjusted. He looked familiar. "Do you know the lady who lives here?"

"She's dead."

"Oh."

"I saw them take her body right out o' here about a month ago."

Olivia swallowed, disappointment rising. "I see. Well, thank you, um…"

"Henry. You're the lady at the thrift shop. I knew your dad."

She nodded. "I remember now. Thank you for letting me know, Henry."

Still clutching the cards, she moved past him, down the walk, and slid into the driver's seat. This explained why the treasures, as she had begun to think of them, had been discarded. Despite the hectic day, she had not stopped wondering about Belinda Marini and the mysterious *J*.

Olivia was just about to drive away when a tapping on her window startled her. Henry's face pressed up against the window, and she lowered it so he could talk to her.

"There was another lady who lived here too. Just thought of that. I think she may have had a son—saw him a couple times. Don't know her name, but I think she moved."

Another lady? Olivia put the truck back into Park. "I'm looking for Belinda Marini. Could that be the other lady's name?"

He pursed his lips. "Might be. The lady who died was named Gladys."

Olivia smiled. *Bingo.* "Henry, do you have any idea where she moved?"

"I think I heard she might be in a care home in St. Martha's. They have a lot of them over there, you know."

She nodded. She knew—her father had lived out his last days in one of them. "Thank you for all this information, Henry."

"What do you think you'll do with it?" he asked.

She took a glance at the cards splayed across the passenger seat, the words "See you next year. Love, J" catching her eyes.

She flashed a look at Henry. "I'm going to try to find her," she said. "And her son."

* * *

On Monday, Jimmy Popchek stepped into the shop, a pair of old fatigues stuffed into his thick-soled boots, determination on his brow. Olivia peered up at him from the inventory spreadsheet she had been trying to complete all morning. Jimmy had served his country but had returned home six months before and taken a reporting gig for the Holly Hills *Dispatch*.

He slapped a notebook on the counter, scattering a stack of flyers for the all-church community bazaar. "Heard you're looking for a missing person." He eyed her laser-like, as if he were a sergeant and she a new recruit.

"At ease, Jimmy."

His shoulders slumped, and he leaned on the counter. "C'mon, Olivia. There hasn't been a good story in this town since that Evans kid drove his Hummer through Joyce Dean's vegetable patch."

She put down her pencil. "Okay, well, I'm looking for a woman named Belinda Marini." She handed him one of the postcards. "I found a whole stack of cards like this, and I'd like to get them back to her. I'd also like to figure out who the sender, *J*, is. I understand he may be her son. If you can help, then I'm all for it."

He jotted the woman's name, her former address, and other notes onto his pad, then straightened. "Jimmy Popchek is on it," he said with a nod of his head. He offered her a salute and marched out the door.

* * *

When Olivia entered the shop the following morning, she found Claire chin-deep in the newspaper.

"Good morning, Claire."

"Says here that Belinda Marini is being desperately sought by the proprietor of the local trinket shop." She looked up, her eyes peeking out over her glasses.

Olivia pulled off her coat and hung it on the rack. "Trinket shop." She sighed. "Is that what this is?"

Claire cleared her throat. "Also says here that the public should be on the lookout for one 'J. Marino,' as if the man's a criminal."

"Maybe he is."

"By the way, your mother called."

"She did? I just left there thirty minutes ago."

"Well, she's been a busy woman since you left. She wanted you to know that she read the story in the paper, and that she's on the case."

Olivia lifted her eyebrows.

"Go ahead and call her if you don't believe me."

Olivia gave Claire a wary glance as she plucked her cell phone from her purse and dialed up her mother. "Mom? You called?"

Her mother sighed into the phone. "Dear, I know you've been very busy at the store, but why didn't you tell me how desperate you were to find Belinda Marini?"

"Mom." Olivia leaned her head back and stared at the ceiling. "Jimmy was embellishing."

"I wanted you to know that I've already filled out a missing person's ad on Craigslist, for Belinda—and her son."

"You're kidding." She swung to look at bespectacled Claire, while still pressing the phone to her ear. "That's brilliant, Mom."

"No, not brilliant, just..." Maryann Young's voice grew wistful. "I just miss your father so much, especially at this time of year, and somehow helping someone else helps me. Do you understand?"

Olivia nodded. "Yes, I think I do."

"Well, I'd best be going. Let's hope for a Christmas miracle, shall we?"

"Absolutely." Olivia said good-bye to her mother and stashed her phone back in her purse.

* * *

At noon, the postman arrived at the shop, only he wasn't their usual mail carrier.

Olivia approached him as he arrived at the counter. "Hello, Randall. It's been a long time."

He removed his hat from his head. "Yes, ma'am. I remember you as a wee one, and here you are, all grown up and a businesswoman at that." He smiled at her. "Your pop would be mighty proud."

Olivia nodded once. "Aw, thank you, Randall. Is there something I can do for you?"

"I heard you're looking for the old woman on Township. Belinda Marini."

Of course. Why had she not thought to talk with the town's mail carriers? "Oh, Randall, do you know where I can find her?"

"Sorry to say, no, ma'am. I'm kickin' myself for not paying better attention to the sweet old woman who was carted away after the other lady died."

"That's okay." She paused. "Do you happen to know if she filled out a change-of-address form?"

He shook his head, his expression forlorn. "Nobody filled one out. But I came here to tell you that I'm going to pay good attention to the mail that comes in—there's lots of cards and letters being processed this time of year. Maybe I'll find some clues for you."

Olivia smiled up at the gentle giant. "Perfect," she said. "That would be perfect."

* * *

Despite a heavy snow the first week in December, the days leading toward Christmas brought in more visitors to the store than Olivia had seen since before summer when graduation parties topped everyone's schedules. While the majority of those who stopped in were looking for good deals on Christmas gifts, a nearly equal number of townsfolk popped in simply to discuss Belinda Marini and her son, the mysterious *J*.

Eighteen-year-old Cat Smythe breezed into the shop in the late afternoon, dropping her backpack by the door and sloughing her jacket onto a chair by the front counter. The high school senior worked nights as a receptionist and hair-sweeper at All Tressed Up, the salon next door. "So I was thinking," she said, plunking her elbows onto the counter. "If *J* sends another postcard soon—what then?"

"I don't know."

Cat frowned. She took her smartphone from her pocket, stretched her arms on the counter, and began frantically working her thumbs over it. "Frustrating that I can't find him on Facebook. I mean, who's not on Facebook?" She glanced up from the screen. "Found anything out about the old lady yet?"

"Not yet. I've called all the large care homes in St. Martha's and no one has ever heard of her. It's strange, really. This isn't New York or Los Angeles or some other big city." She didn't add, *you know, places I'd like to see someday.* "This is Holly Hills. Surely we can keep better track of our people than this!"

Cat slid off the chair and motioned to Olivia. "C'mon."

"C'mon where?"

"Let's go to Belinda's house and look for clues."

Olivia's mouth dropped open. Then she laughed. "I have a business to run. And you, you have a job to get to."

Cat tugged on her arm. "It'll only take a few minutes. C'mon. Let's go."

* * *

Olivia gasped. "It's beautiful."

Cat pulled into the narrow driveway of Belinda Marini's house, a smile across her face. She peered at the house. "Wonder who did it."

"Henry, maybe?"

Cat laughed. "The old neighbor?"

Olivia just shrugged and popped open the door. A crisp front of air licked her cheeks as she stepped out of the car to view the lights displayed on Mrs. Marini's house.

He goaded her on with a nod of his head. "It's the name and phone number of Mrs. Marini's conservator, a Miss Charlene Vander."

A sigh escaped her. "Wha…? How? You know where she is?"

"She saw the article in the paper and came by the house. But that's all I could get from her. Wouldn't tell me nothing other than she, too, is looking for the old woman's kin. I figured you could call her though. She'd talk to you."

"Why would she talk to me?"

He blushed. "'Cause you're a pretty lady, not some old man with nothing but time on his hands."

She shook her head. "Don't ever sell yourself short like that, Henry." She scanned the pretty display lighting up the abandoned house. "You use your time very well, I'd say."

Cat, older and wiser than her eighteen years, chimed in too. "You're the coolest old man I know."

* * *

Olivia's mother sat across from her at the old pine table in the dining room, focused with precision on her laptop screen. If Olivia had not witnessed for herself her mother's deep sadness since her father's passing, she would have never believed it. She would never admit it to another soul, but her mother was the reason she never left Holly Hills. But now her mother looked up at her with life in her eyes that Olivia had not seen for over a year. "Think I may have located Belinda Marini."

"What? How did…?"

She turned the laptop enough so Olivia could view the screen. "I found Charlene Vander, the conservator, on

LinkedIn—can't believe I hadn't thought of that before—and see there?" She pointed to Charlene's profile and photo. "She has patients all over the county, many of them in small board and care homes—not the larger, well-known convalescent hospitals we all know. I looked up each one and…wait just a second…"

She pulled back the laptop and typed furiously, then turned it toward Olivia again. "This one right here—Sunrise Home Care—two boroughs over, is for patients without next of kin."

"She *has* next of kin—she has *J.*"

"Obviously Charlene doesn't know his whereabouts either. Or she wouldn't have gone hunting around the old woman's home."

"If only she'd return my phone call…"

Her mother shrugged. "Maybe she's busy. It appears that she travels a lot, plus it's the holidays. She very well may not get to you until January."

"Well then," Olivia said. "Guess I'm going to pay Sunrise Home Care a visit tomorrow."

Maryann Young shut her laptop and reached across the table to give her daughter's hand a squeeze. "And I'm going with you."

* * *

Unlike the neighboring houses all wrapped in clapboard, Sunrise Care Home was built of beautiful red brick. Red poinsettias in window boxes and two gigantic pine wreaths on the doors welcomed visitors.

A heavyset woman stuffed into paisley scrubs answered the door. "May I help you?"

Olivia smiled. "We'd like to see Belinda Marini."

The woman's wan face brightened. "Well!"

Maryann leaned forward. "May we?"

The woman blinked hard and gave her head a quick shake. "Come in, come in."

Done with the formalities, she led them through a small, dark living room. Olivia longed to run to the windows and throw open the drapes.

The woman led them through the first doorway on the right side of the narrow hallway. "Belinda," she said, her voice like a radio announcer's, "you have guests, young lady."

The old woman's eyes slid toward them, but her head barely moved. Her mouth hung open as she watched them in silence.

The nurse squeezed Belinda's feet. "These ladies came here to visit you, Belinda. Isn't that nice?"

One side of Belinda's mouth pulled up, as if trying to form a smile. The other side drooped.

The nurse turned to Olivia. "She's had a stroke, poor thing, so she can't speak."

Maryann sat in an armchair near the foot of the bed and motioned for her daughter to take the hardback seat nearest to Belinda.

Olivia opened her mouth but couldn't quite think of what to say to the stranger who lay in the bed in front of her.

"Tell her about the cards, darlin'," her mother prompted.

Olivia flipped her gaze toward Mrs. Marini. "I have something of yours." She opened her purse and pulled out the stack of postcards, wrapped in a festive bow that she'd plucked from her store's supplies. She held out the cards, her hand hovering over the woman's thick brown blanket. "Here. I found these and thought maybe you would want them back."

The old woman groaned, and her brows drooped.

The nurse walked to the other side of the bed and reached across for the postcards. "Oh, honey, let me take them for her." She looked at Mrs. Marini and spoke in that loud voice again. "The nice lady brought you some postcards, and oh my, they are beautiful! Such festive colors and places. I think I will post them around your room so you can look at them."

The woman groaned a second time, and Olivia frowned. Though she didn't know exactly what she had expected to find, it wasn't...this. And yet hadn't her father gone through a very similar decline? Hadn't she and her mother watched their hero lose his strength while all they could do was sit by his side and pray? She glanced again at Mrs. Marini. Surely she should try harder to make a connection with the dear woman. "Mrs. Marini, I'm so glad to have found you. No one seemed to know where you had gone—your neighbor, Henry, was concerned."

The old woman stared at her, her face expressionless. It unnerved Olivia, but she pressed on. "I noticed that your son, *J*, sends you postcards every year."

At Olivia's words, Mrs. Marini's eyes grew wide.

Olivia rested her hand on the woman's, and spoke slowly. "Does *J* know you're here?"

Mrs. Marini's lips moved, but no sound came out.

The nurse leaned closer to her and spoke. "Why, Belinda Marini, you've been holding out on us. You never told me you had a son! Does he know you're here?"

Finally, the woman shook her head emphatically. *No.*

* * *

Olivia bit back a sigh, and held the phone to her ear.

"Like I told you before, Olivia," Charlene Vander said, "I'm dealing with a woman's privacy here and I'm not supposed to divulge anything."

"But I don't understand. She obviously has a son with the initial *J*. Her neighbor Henry has seen him a few times."

"Unfortunately, the cleaning service stripped the house of nearly everything before I was called onto the scene. I *did* try to trace Belinda's family through her last known address, but nobody there had heard of her."

"But surely someone knew her..."

"Look. I did what I could. When I saw the house had lights, I investigated to see if anyone from her family had shown up." She heaved a sigh. "I can't spend any more time on this. I'm just...I'm just overwhelmed with cases at the moment."

After another moment of conversation, Olivia hung up the phone in silence.

Claire watched her over the rim of her reading glasses. "Dead end?"

"At least she took my call." She frowned. "If only Mrs. Marini hadn't fallen asleep so quickly after we arrived, maybe she would have been able to at least give me a clue to her son's whereabouts."

"Did this Charlene tell you anything? Anything at all?"

"She confirmed that she is Belinda Marini's conservator, but because I'm not the next of kin, she wouldn't tell me much."

The door to the shop swung open then, sweeping in a burst of cold. Randall stood zipped up to his chin in his postal parka, the furry flaps of his trooper cap protecting his ears. "Mornin', ladies."

"For goodness' sake, Randall," said Claire. "Step in her and shut that door."

Randall hurried toward the counter, something in his hands. A postcard. A big, colorful postcard. "Miss Olivia. Look what we got here."

Olivia sucked in a breath and reached across the counter to take the postcard that Randall so eagerly offered. "It's from J, isn't it?"

He nodded, those earflaps bouncing. "Yes. Yes, it is."

Claire slid over to look. "What's it say?"

Olivia let her eyes run across the now-familiar handwriting, then looked up. "He's coming home."

Randall pulled the cap off of his head and held it to his chest. "You don't say. Well. That's some good news right there."

"It's amazing news, Randall." She flipped over the card. "Wow, he's coming from Tahiti. I can't tell what's more clear in the picture—the water or the sky. "

Claire glanced outside at the murky day. "That man must really love his mother to come here from there." Behind her, the phone rang, and she pushed away from the counter. "I'll get that."

Olivia continued to finger the postcard. "He says he'll be here on Christmas Eve. That's soon."

Randall watched her, but his droopy eyes perked upward, as if on alert. "What're you gonna do, Miss Olivia? You can't let that fella come home and find his mama's home empty."

She nodded, her momentary elation fizzling. "You're absolutely right. Somebody has to meet him there and give him the news...but what news can we give him?"

Claire held out the phone while covering the mouthpiece with her other hand. "It's Charlene again!"

Olivia shushed her with a wave of her hand, then took the phone. "Hello, Charlene?" She glanced up at Randall and Claire, who stared at her with their mouths stuck open. "I've got some news for you."

* * *

"Is it true? Did you find the old woman?"

Olivia swung around at the sound of Paula Harris's voice. Paula showed up very early once per week, hoping to find that "one" thing that would make her rich on eBay. It was already Christmas Eve *eve*, so perhaps this time around, Paula was just on the hunt for a special gift.

Olivia nodded. "Indeed we did."

Paula clapped her hands together as if she'd just found a Coach purse without a tear or stain. "Wonderful! It's on the front page, but you never know how that Jimmy Popchek does his research."

Olivia raised an eyebrow. Considering Jimmy hadn't stepped into the shop in weeks, it was a valid question. Ever since learning of *J*'s impending arrival, she'd been less than forthcoming about that news. Claire blew in through the door with a copy of the newspaper tucked under her arm. She dropped it onto the counter and began peeling off her gloves. "You made the news again, I see."

"That's what I heard. Only Jimmy never called me."

Claire snorted. "Aw, you know Jimmy. Always sniffing out the drama. The boy just may make it big as an investigative reporter someday."

Olivia glanced over at Paula to make sure she was deeply ensconced in some retail therapy. She kept her eyes on her while whispering to Claire. "I've decided to go and meet him myself. I don't want the whole town showing up as I'm giving the poor old gent the news."

Claire nodded. "Good idea. But I'll go with you, and make sure Henry is there as well. Just to be safe."

"There's only one flight coming into the regional tomorrow, so my guess is he'll be at the house by three o'clock. We'll be closed by then. Want to meet me there?"

Claire gave her one forceful nod. "I'm on it."

* * *

On this eve before Christmas, Claire, Olivia's mother, and Henry gathered with Olivia behind Henry's expansive bay window for the mysterious *J* to arrive. The four of them sat in peaceful near-silence as they waited to reunite a mother and son.

"Would anyone like another biscuit?" Henry asked, offering a tray of iced Christmas cookies for the third time since they arrived.

Maryann reached over. "I don't mind if I do."

Henry returned to his seat, a satisfied smile etching his face.

A red car pulled up the street, slowing as it reached the driveway of the home where Gladys and Belinda once lived.

Claire leaned forward. "That's him," she whispered.

Olivia let out a deep sigh and stood. "Okay. Here I go." She pulled on her gloves and then her coat before stepping onto Henry's porch, with her entourage following closely behind. But as the car door opened and the man stepped out, Olivia stopped. Claire and her mother careened into her back, nearly knocking her over.

Maryann leaned over Olivia's right shoulder. "He's far too young to be *J*, don't you think?"

Henry piped up, "That's him, all right. Only saw him a couple of times, but he was tall."

"Tall?" Claire asked, never taking her eyes off of him. "He's downright hunky, if you ask me."

Olivia shushed her.

They all stood there, watching the tanned man take the porch steps two at a time, then rap on the front door with his bare knuckles. Olivia felt Claire shove into her back—this time on purpose. "Olivia! *Stat!*"

Olivia frowned. This wasn't how she'd envisioned the scenario. In her mind, *J* was a man of at least fifty—maybe even sixty. Touristy clothes, balding on top, grey above the ears. Now as she looked across the driveway at the broad-shouldered man with sandy brown hair, she mentally tried to rewrite her script.

Maryann nudged her. "Go on, honey."

Olivia began to descend the steps when a husky voice interrupted her mental revisions.

"Excuse me," he said.

Olivia stopped and raised her chin as the man closed the space between them in a few giant steps.

The eyes that searched her face were beautiful and clear but looked oh so tired. "I'm looking for Belinda Marini. Would you happen to know where she has gone?"

"You must be *J*."

Surprise lit those tired eyes. His brows rose and a slight smile lifted his lips as he reached out his hand. "I'm Jacob Reed," he said, shaking her gloved hand. "And you are?"

"I'm Olivia...and I'm also a bit confused."

Gently he let her go. "I don't understand."

She pulled in a deep breath. "You see, I've been waiting for you." She glanced behind her. "We've all been waiting for you, or rather, for Mrs. Marini's son."

He watched her intently.

"But, well, you seem too, um..."

He broke in. "Is she all right?"

"Yes. Well, yes and no. She became ill and had to move." Olivia cocked her head to one side. "Who are you, exactly?"

A crease formed between Jacob's eyes. "Belinda Marini is my grandmother, but she raised me, so I always think of her as my mother. Can you tell me where she is?"

Maryann rushed forward. "Her grandson?" She placed her hands on Olivia's arms as if holding her out on display. "My daughter knows where your grandmother is staying now and she can take you there. She didn't want you to find your mother's home abandoned."

He smiled, his eyes imploring. "That's very kind of you. I'm...I'm very grateful. So you'll take me to her?"

Olivia nodded. "Absolutely."

* * *

In ten short minutes, Olivia learned that Jacob Reed was an international business consultant who spent as much time in the air as on the ground. His grandmother, a retired teacher, had lived with him in upstate New York until her health grew too weak, and he was no longer comfortable about leaving her alone. About that time, a former student of hers, Gladys Macomb, invited her to live with her. It had never occurred to him that the much younger Gladys would pass away before his grandmother.

"Can I ask you something?" she asked when they stopped at one of the few lights in town.

"Certainly."

"Why do your postcards always say 'See you next year,' if you don't actually come home for Christmas?"

He laughed. "Because I always come home—or wherever 'mother' is—on New Year's Day." His eyes twinkled when he reminisced. "It's always been our little joke."

* * *

When they entered Sunrise Home Care, the drapes had been drawn back to allow in hazy light from the afternoon sun. The room, dark and foreboding the last time, had blossomed into a lovely entryway for visitors.

"Please wait here," a young woman said.

Jacob shoved both hands into his pockets, his glance bouncing around the room. Olivia wished there was something she could do to ease his trepidation at seeing his grandmother in this state.

Suddenly, Jacob turned to her. "I'm grateful for your concern." He shook his head. "I've been trying to reach my grandmother and Gladys for weeks—in between trips—and couldn't understand why they weren't answering the phone." His voice broke. "She's my only family."

As he said the words, Olivia's heart clenched. "Charlene Vander—she's your mother's conservator—well, she said that a cleaning service had emptied the house of most of its contents before she was called in. With no apparent next of kin…"

He sighed. "She was shipped off here like a ward of the state."

The young nurse reentered the room. "Mrs. Marini is ready to see you now."

Jacob started to move forward, then stopped and looked at Olivia. "Come with me."

"You sure?"

He nodded.

Soft Christmas music played as they entered Belinda Marini's room. Her eyes were closed, but she wore a faint smile on her face. Olivia watched as Jacob walked quickly toward his grandmother, bent down, and kissed her forehead.

At his touch, the woman awoke and let out a gasp, then a joyous cry. She reached her arms to him, and he stayed bent, letting his only kin hold him close.

"Mother," he whispered.

"My… Jacob," she whispered back.

The young nurse's mouth fell open. She looked from Belinda to Jacob to Olivia, tears forming. "It's a… miracle," she said. "She doesn't speak!"

* * *

As Jacob and Belinda continued their reunion, Olivia retreated to the living room of the quaint brick care facility. There she found Henry, Claire, and her mother—her own personal entourage—waiting in a quiet circle next to the room's picture window. Cat Smythe and Jimmy Popchek had somehow learned of the reunion and joined the group in the living room.

Claire spoke. "Don't be mad, but we eavesdropped."

Olivia laughed. "I'm not mad."

Maryann stood and wrapped her arms around her daughter. "I'd say this is one beautiful Christmas Eve."

Olivia leaned into her mother's embrace. "My best yet."

Jacob stepped into the room then, his frame filling the doorway. All eyes turned upward, but his gaze was affixed on Olivia.

"I can't thank you enough."

She shook her head. "Please. It was the whole town, really. All of us...I'm..." She looked at the five happy faces surrounding her. "We're so glad you found each other again."

He smiled, this time his eyes looking far less tired than they had earlier. He took in the small room full of people, then let his gaze travel to the warmth of lights filling the street, that smile staying on his face.

Henry was the first to speak. "This old town sure does come alive at Christmas, don't it?"

Jacob nodded. "Indeed it does."

"Do you think a world traveler like yourself could learn to love a place like Holly Hills?" Olivia's mother asked.

A slow smile stretched across his face. "I'll have to start my travels again eventually, but I'm due a nice long break. And Holly Hills definitely holds promise." He touched Olivia on the shoulder. "What do you think?"

Olivia glanced out the home's picture window toward the white, twinkling lights illuminating the neighborhood. "I'd have to agree," she said. "A hundred percent."

A STRANGER'S VISIT TO THE LIGHTHOUSE

Marilyn Turk

Christmas Eve, 1895
Little Bay Lighthouse, Maine

You won't be gone long, will you, John?" Isabel's hands rested atop the mound of her stomach as she stood in the open door to the lighthouse keeper's home.

"Don't you fret, Isabel. I'll be back long before dusk. I just have a few errands to do in town before meeting your mother on the noon train." He pulled her close as possible and kissed her forehead. "I've got to be back to light the lamps, you know." Peering down at her with tender eyes, he gave her a wink.

"Yes, I know." She forced her lips upward into a smile. "Please be careful."

"I will. You take care of our little one while I'm gone, you hear?" John glanced down at her bulging middle, kissed her again, then turned and walked down to the shore where the lighthouse skiff was tied up.

Isabel's heart twisted as he got in the boat and rowed away. She loved their little island home, but sometimes the loneliness was difficult to bear. *It's only a few miles to the mainland*, she chided herself, but the same unsettled feeling she got every time John went for supplies crept through her again.

She lifted her gaze to the white lighthouse standing sentinel on the bluff above the water's edge. Not only did it represent John's position, but it was also John's pride and joy. Her heart filled with admiration for his dedication to keeping the light burning, the lantern polished, and the tower clean, a routine that had earned him several keeper awards. Many mariners owed their lives to his faithful commitment.

Isabel closed the door, leaned against it, then sighed. *Relax. You're just overly emotional these days.* She massaged her round middle. The baby would be here soon, in about two weeks, if she'd calculated right. Perhaps once the baby rested snug in its cradle, she'd stop letting her fears run away with her. Thank God John was bringing Mother back with him. Isabel missed the company of other women, and it would be especially nice to have her mother with her. When Isabel went into labor, Mother's experience and capable hands could handle any problems that came up.

A ripple of excitement coursed through her at the prospect of showing her mother the cottage. This would be Mother's first visit to the island since John became keeper of the Little Bay Lighthouse. Isabel had worked hard to make their home as warm and inviting as the home where she'd been raised. She'd sewn ruffled muslin curtains for the windows and crocheted pillows for the furniture, giving the cottage a cozy feeling just right for her and John. And the baby.

As if on cue, the baby kicked. "Soon, little one. Soon you'll get to see your new home yourself." A smile eased onto her face as she spoke loving words to the baby. "Your daddy teases me for talking to you, but I know you're listening." She patted her stomach and the child inside. "Just wait until you see the lovely crib Daddy made for you."

A pleasant aroma wafted into the room from the kitchen, reminding her she had a pie in the oven, made with the island's blueberries, which she'd canned last summer. She plodded to the stove and bent over to retrieve the pie, then placed it on the table beside the stove to cool. As she straightened, she placed her hands on the small of her back. Two more weeks. Could she carry all this weight that much longer?

* * *

John leaned backward as he pulled the oars through the water. The tide was coming in, aiding his progress to the mainland. He raised his eyes to the sky, the clear blue of a cold winter's day. *Thank God, the weather is nice today.*

He hated leaving Isabel alone, especially with the birth so near. She tired so easily lately, yet seldom asked for his help, determined to stay strong even when he knew her fears lay just below the surface. If only he could keep her from worrying. After losing the first child before it was born, Isabel feared she might not be able to carry a child all the way. But this time, by the grace of God, the child was almost here. They'd prayed for a healthy child, and soon their prayers would be answered.

"Lord, be with her and comfort her while I'm away," he uttered aloud. A breeze blew across the water, ruffling the surface, as if in answer.

* * *

Isabel sank into the rocking chair by the fireplace, then pulled a shirt out of the basket of mending beside the chair. Retrieving a needle and thread from her sewing kit, she began to work on one of John's shirts. His buttons often ripped off or his shirts got torn when he snagged them while cleaning the prisms on the lantern. Mr. Strathmore, the lighthouse supervisor, was very particular about the keepers' appearances, so she stayed busy mending John's clothing, especially his official uniform. She certainly didn't want to be the reason John got marked off at Mr. Strathmore's next inspection.

After a while, she lowered the needle and thread, resting the shirt in her lap. She smiled at the little fir John cut for their Christmas tree, adorned with strands of cranberries and ornaments she and John made. It was fun crocheting the snowflakes, but she was especially proud of the crocheted angel perched on the top.

Isabel's gaze traveled down to the little Nativity scene beneath the tree. Her heart swelled with pride as she recalled the long hours John put into carving each piece, the care he'd taken to shape the infant in the manger. She'd oohed and aahed over each of the lifelike characters, amazed at her husband's workmanship.

"Nothing but the best for the Lord," he'd said, and it was obvious he strived for perfection as he used his God-given talent.

She tied a knot in the thread at the base of the button, thankful she'd married such a kind, godly man. Thank God, he hadn't taken "no" for an answer when he proposed the first time. She smiled, remembering why John decided to become a light keeper in the first place. Her refusal to marry a sailor prompted him to give up his dream of being captain of his own ship in the navy, joining the lighthouse service instead. Isabel felt the familiar pang of guilt that accompanied John's sacrifice for her.

But the life of a lighthouse keeper's wife hadn't turned out as she'd expected either, especially now that they lived so far from their families. The thought of spending Christmas without the rest of her relatives threatened to dampen her holiday spirit. But fortunately Mother had agreed to come, even though she'd miss sharing the holiday with her other daughters and their families.

Isabel finished the mending and pushed herself out of the chair. She shivered and pulled her shawl around her shoulders. Was it getting colder in the house or was it just her body's erratic temperatures lately—hot one moment and cold the next? She threw another log on the fire and then went to the stove to put the teakettle on. As she waited for the whistle of steam, she glanced out the window and gasped.

* * *

John kept an eye on the darkening sky to the west of town. As he hurried out of the hardware store, he frowned at the building clouds slowly snuffing out the sunshine of the morning. Where had those come from? Mr. Thompson glanced up from carving meat as John entered the butcher shop.

"Mornin,' John." He nodded toward the window. "It gettin' darker out there, or is it my imagination?"

"It's getting darker, I hate to say. Looks like we have a storm coming."

"Maybe we'll have snow for Christmas, eh?" Mr. Thompson's accent gave away his Canadian roots.

"Perhaps. Only I wish the storm would hold off awhile longer. If it's a bad one, I don't want to be caught in it."

"So you should go ahead and leave now, eh?"

John shook his head. "Can't. Isabel's mother is arriving on the noon train, and I have to fetch her. She's spending Christmas with us."

"That so? I'm sure Isabel will be happy to have her mum." Mr. Thompson wrapped up some steaks in butcher paper and wiped his hands on his apron. "How's your wife doing? 'Bout time for the babe, isn't it?"

"Isabel's fine, thank you. She says the baby is due in two more weeks."

"Her mother's staying until after the baby's born, I hope? We men aren't much use with babies. When Gretchen had all ours, she and her mum shooed me out of the house. Fine with me too. I was always afraid I'd drop one of the little 'uns or do something wrong."

John observed the large man's hands, big as the hams hanging behind him. He could no doubt hold an infant in one of them. He couldn't contain his chuckle, imagining the big man afraid of holding a little baby.

"I'm thankful her mother agreed to come. Isabel's been pretty lonely without her family, especially at this time of year. Plus, I think she's nervous about...being alone at a time like this.

Neither of us is"—heat flooded his face—"you know…experienced."

"You best stay out of their way too. Just jump when they say jump." Mr. Thompson pointed a finger at him.

"Isn't that what we do anyway, Mr. Thompson? To keep our women happy?"

Both men laughed out loud. Then Mr. Thompson crossed his arms. "So what can I do for you today, John? Need a ham?"

"Certainly do. We hope to have it for Christmas dinner."

"Here ya go." Mr. Thompson passed the wrapped ham across the counter. "And here, take some of this sausage. Smoked it myself."

John reached in his pocket for his money, but the big man held up his hand.

"No. It's a gift. Merry Christmas. May God bless you and the missus with a healthy baby."

"Thank you. Merry Christmas to you and your family as well." John tipped his cap, then left the store and headed for the train station.

When he reached the depot, the train hadn't arrived yet. John paced the platform and pulled out his pocket watch. Fifteen minutes late. Couldn't the train be early today?

He pictured Isabel waiting and watching for him at the window, creases of concern marring her sweet face. She was so excited about Christmas and had gone to such effort to decorate their little home for the holiday. He couldn't bear seeing her disappointment if things didn't go as she'd planned. She'd worry herself sick if he didn't get back today, and she certainly didn't need something else to be concerned about.

"Just got a wire about heavy snow up the line slowing things down," John overheard the clerk at the ticket window tell the man in front of him.

As John stared down the tracks, strong winds began to blow. John pulled up his collar and closed the top of his coat, as did the others waiting on the platform. He glanced at the clock hanging above the depot door. Thirty minutes late.

Finally, John heard the train whistle in the distance, and he blew out a sigh of relief. As the train rolled in, the wind howled like a wounded animal. Snow began falling in huge wet drops while the train huffed and puffed into the station, its giant wheels squealing to a stop.

"John! Over here!"

John followed the voice and saw his plump mother-in-law descending the steps of one of the cars. He rushed over to help her down.

"Welcome, Mother Harris. Did you have a pleasant journey?"

"I'm so glad to see you, John. We stopped several times to shovel snow off the tracks. Thank God, it's not bad here."

Not yet, but taking the boat back out in this weather was out of the question. John could see the water from where he stood, the rolling, angry sea already too much for the skiff to handle. He couldn't take the chance of the small boat capsizing in the rough waves.

"I'm afraid we can't leave now, Mother Harris." He grabbed her suitcase. "We'll have to wait until the storm passes. I pray that will be soon." Motioning across the street, he said, "Meanwhile, let's get something hot to drink in the hotel dining room."

* * *

Isabel gaped at the black clouds creeping toward the lighthouse while frigid fingers of wind slipped through the cracks around the window. Frothy waves churned up the unsuspecting sea and sent them crashing into the shore, splashing against the rocks. Isabel gripped the edges of her shawl and hugged herself.

Oh no. Not today. Not a storm on Christmas Eve. The clock chimed once, drawing her attention to the mantle. *One o'clock.* Mother's train should have arrived, and John would have met her by now. What if they were in the boat in this weather? Her chest tightened at a vision of the skiff fighting turbulent waves.

Shoving her worrisome thoughts aside, she checked the large pot of vegetable soup simmering on the back of the stove. As she lifted the lid, she inhaled the rich aroma of onions and carrots, then stirred the contents. John loved her good, hearty soup. She imagined the smile on his face when he returned to be welcomed home with a hot bowl of broth. She removed the towel from the bread she'd made yesterday and cut several thick slices. Everything would be ready when they arrived. If only they could beat the storm.

She poured another cup of hot tea, then returned to the parlor and placed the cup on a side table beside the large family Bible. As the storm advanced and light inside the house faded, Isabel lit the kerosene lamp so she could see to read. The Bible was marked with passages of comfort she went to when fear threatened her peace. Her favorite Scriptures were in the book of Psalms that promised God's presence and comfort and told her to "fear not."

How she yearned to immerse herself in those words. She closed her eyes and recited them from memory as gale-force winds blew against the house, whistling through the cracks.

"What time I am afraid, I will trust in thee."

Icy rain began to pelt the windows.

Opening her eyes, she flipped to the bookmark in Isaiah. "Fear not: for I am with thee."

A voice inside her head said "Trust Me."

Yes, Lord, I want to.

What could she do to keep busy? Isabel reviewed a mental list of things she'd meant to accomplish before Christmas arrived. Make the pie—done. Cook soup—done. Mend John's clothes—done. Dust the furniture—done. Finish John's present—oh! She'd almost forgotten.

Isabel went into the bedroom and opened a trunk that rested at the end of the bed. She removed several blankets before she found what she was looking for. As she took out the bottom blanket, she unfolded it. Inside lay a knit cap, gloves, and scarf, made of dark-blue woolen yarn. She ran her fingers over the soft material, feeling its warmth. John certainly needed these things in their Maine winters. His old ones were so worn out that even mending didn't help.

There were just a few finishing touches to put on her handiwork and she planned to do so while he was gone today. Returning to the parlor, she stole a glance at the window. The wind howled, and sleet pinged against the house. Surely John had stayed in town to wait out the storm. Would he have risked his and her mother's safety to get back, just so she wouldn't be afraid? She shook her head. No. He was the one with the level head.

As she settled back in her rocker with her knitting, she began to pray for John and for her mother. She prayed for her sisters and their families, for sailors at sea, and for anyone else caught in the storm. Then she prayed for the baby. She hoped for a boy, a John Junior. She envisioned a little mirror image of her husband trotting around behind him. She smiled at the picture in her mind, her heart warming with joy. Yet she'd be thankful for a healthy baby girl as well.

As she rocked, her eyelids grew heavy. Her hands dropped in her lap as the rhythm of the storm droned a curious lullaby.

* * *

"It looks like we'll have to stay here for the night." John turned from the window to face his mother-in-law.

"Oh dear. I was afraid of that." Mother Harris cast an anxious glance out the window of the hotel dining room as she held a hot cup of tea. "I hate for Isabel to be alone tonight."

"I do too." John clenched his fingers into fists and rammed them into his pockets. "We have no choice. One thing I learned from my sailing days is to stay in port when the weather is dangerous."

"Yes, of course. I certainly don't relish the thought of being in a boat in this storm. Do you think Isabel will be all right? Is she getting along okay with the baby's time so near?"

John nodded. "She's well, just tired. Eager for the baby to be born."

"She's wanted a baby so long." The older woman stood and smoothed her long skirt. "Are you certain they have enough rooms tonight? The hotel may be full with Christmas visitors or stranded travelers like us."

"I'll check at the front desk." John looked toward the lobby. "If they only have one room, you can have it and I'll sleep downstairs in a chair. Wait here until I find out." He strode over to the desk and after a few moments with the clerk, returned.

"We're in luck. Got the last two rooms—well, mine's more of a broom closet, but it's shelter." John forced a smile.

"My dear, I don't believe in luck. It's God's providence we're here and not out in the storm." Mother Harris nodded.

"You're right. If we'd been in the boat when the storm hit, we'd be in serious trouble."

"I do hope Isabel gets some rest tonight and doesn't stay up worrying about us. She's always been such a worrier."

"I hope so too. I haven't left her overnight by herself since we moved to the island."

"I'm sure she's capable of taking care of herself. She won't do anything that will jeopardize the safety of the baby."

Alarm slammed into John's gut with nearly the same force as the gale. He clapped his hand over his mouth.

"What is it, John?" His mother-in-law's brow wrinkled in concern.

"The light! I won't be there to light the lamps. I hope she doesn't attempt to do that herself."

"Oh my. Do you really think she would?"

"She knows how important it is, to me and to anyone out at sea, to have the light burning. She's accompanied me up the tower in the past when I lit the wicks, but not since she's gotten so large with the baby." John didn't want Isabel's mother to know just how unsafe it could be for Isabel to climb the narrow, winding stairs in her condition. *God, if she tries and falls, I'll never forgive myself.*

Mother Harris laid her hand on John's arm. "John, we need to pray for Isabel."

John bowed his head as she prayed. "Dear Lord, please take care of Isabel and send Your comfort during this time. Protect her, guard her with Your angels, and keep both her and the baby safe. Amen."

John lifted his head and gave his mother-in-law a hug. "Thank you. I felt a sense of peace when you prayed, and I trust that Isabel will too."

* * *

Isabel lifted her head, groggy from her nap. As her eyes came into focus, she jerked awake. What time was it? She scanned the room, dark now save for the glow from the kerosene lamp. Was it evening already?

She squinted to see the time on the clock. *Five o'clock.* A rush of anxiety quickened her pulse. John and Mother weren't here. And they wouldn't be arriving now that it was dark. She was alone…on Christmas Eve. This was not what she'd planned. She'd envisioned sitting around their small dining table with John and Mother, enjoying hot soup and fresh bread, laughing and talking, relishing each other's company.

She might as well remove the soup from the heat. No one would be joining her tonight. As she moved her body, stiff from sitting so long, to the kitchen, she tried to see outside, but there was nothing but darkness. Daytime ended early this time of year, plus the storm had removed all light. She paused and listened. Save for the ticking of the clock, it was quiet. The rain and sleet had stopped. *Thank God, the storm has passed.*

She ladled some soup into a bowl for herself as her stomach growled its impatience.

"All right, little one. I suppose you're hungry too." She patted her tummy. Carrying the bowl, she walked to the table and set it down. She grabbed the back of the wooden chair to pull it out, then stopped and tilted her head. What was that noise?

Was someone knocking at the door? Yes, that was knocking. Her heart raced, beating wildly in her chest. Could it be John? Oh my, they did come! They'd made it!

She hurried to the door and unbolted the latch. She pulled it open, ready to leap into John's arms, but he wasn't there. Her hand flew to her mouth, and she sucked in a breath.

Standing in front of her was a man she'd never seen before. His soaked hat pulled over his ears, he shivered from the cold.

"Ma'am, I'm sorry to bother you, but my boat wrecked on the rocks below. I saw the light from your house and hoped to find someone here who could help me."

Isabel shuddered as cold wind forced its way through the open door. She studied the stranger. She'd never let a man in the house without John there. But the poor man was freezing. Where else could he go? How could she send him away, knowing she could give him shelter? What if John was in the same situation and sought help? She hoped someone would be compassionate enough to let him in.

"My husband's not here right now. He went into town today for supplies, but he's been delayed by the storm." The man lifted his clear blue eyes to her, appealing, and her heart went out to him. She didn't know why, but she wasn't afraid of him. "Please come in out of the cold."

"Thank you, ma'am. You are very kind." He entered and stood dripping by the door.

"Let me take your hat and coat." Isabel reached for the wet garments. "Warm yourself by the fire."

"Thank you." The stranger walked to the fireplace and glanced back at her. "Would you like me to throw on another log? The fire is quite low."

"Oh yes, please. I needed to do that. It will probably be much colder tonight." Isabel watched the tall, blond-haired man bend over to pick up a log from the pile beside the fireplace.

He threw on the wood, then stoked the fire with the poker. "There, that should do it." He brushed off his hands.

Isabel gestured to the chair beside the fireplace. "Please sit down and get comfortable. Have you been out in this weather a long time?"

The man nodded and smiled. "Quite a while. Perhaps I should introduce myself. My name is Gabe Goodman."

"Isabel. Isabel Morgan. My husband is John." She settled on the sofa.

"I've heard of him. He was in the navy, wasn't he?"

Isabel raised her eyebrows. "Yes, how did you know?"

"We have a mutual friend."

"Oh?" Isabel cocked her head. "I'm afraid I don't know many of John's navy mates." She studied Mr. Goodman. Warmth and sincerity radiated from him. Why did she feel so comfortable around him, as if he was a friend and not a stranger?

He scanned the room, then motioned to the Christmas tree. "What charming Christmas decorations you have. I especially like the Nativity scene."

Isabel followed his gaze to look at the tree "Thank you. John carved it." A deep sigh escaped from her.

"Is everything all right?" Mr. Goodman's face registered concern.

"Yes. Well, I hope so." Should she confide in this stranger? "I'm just a bit worried about my husband and my mother. John was supposed to meet my mother's train and bring her back here today. They haven't returned yet, and with this storm..."

"You're worried something has happened to them?" He finished her sentence for her.

Isabel nodded, then lowered her eyes, fighting the tears that threatened to form.

"I'm sure they're fine. Your husband knows the sea and wouldn't take any chances that would harm your mother."

She raised her head to look at Mr. Goodman. "I know you're right. I shouldn't worry so."

Mr. Goodman pointed to the open Bible on the side table and nodded. "I'm sure you know the Good Book tells you not to worry or be afraid."

"Yes, I've been reading it today, telling myself to 'fear not,' as it says. Perhaps I'm just selfish. I really wanted to spend Christmas Eve with my family, with John and Mother."

"That's a normal desire for most people. Nothing to feel guilty about."

"What about you, Mr. Goodman? Do you have family?" Isabel bit her tongue. She didn't mean to pry into his personal life.

Mr. Goodman chuckled and spread out his arms. "I have a very large family. Seems like I have family everywhere I go."

What a curious thing to say. "So you have relatives near here? I expect they're worried about you too."

Mr. Goodman lifted his face and sniffed. "Something smells wonderful."

"Oh my goodness. I'm so sorry! I forgot to offer you anything." Isabel jumped to her feet. "I have some fresh-made soup. In fact, I was about to have some when you arrived. Would you like a bowl?"

"Warm soup—just what a body needs in this cold weather! I'd greatly appreciate it, that is, if you can spare any. But please don't go to any trouble for me."

"It's quite all right." She tried to hurry across the room, but her weight slowed her. From the corner of her eye, Isabel saw Mr. Goodman watching her as she crossed the room. He stood and followed her to the kitchen. Isabel's face warmed, embarrassed by her clumsy gait.

"Children are a gift from God." A broad smile spread across the man's face. "Your first?"

Her breath caught. She forced a swallow and nodded. *Was that a lie?* Her first baby was already with the Lord. She reached for a bowl and filled it with soup, placed it on a plate, then laid a slice of bread beside it, her back to her guest.

"May I pray for you?" Mr. Goodman offered.

How did he know her fears? Isabel nodded and bowed her head. "Please."

Mr. Goodman placed his hand on her shoulder. Ordinarily, she'd recoil from a stranger's touch, but instead of fear, his hand released warmth through her. "Lord, we know that You are with Isabel and the baby, and You will take care of them both. We also know You are with John and Mrs. Harris, and You will protect them as well."

Isabel turned to face him and handed him the soup and bread. Tears filled her eyes as she said, "Thank you." Something he'd said piqued her curiosity, but she couldn't remember what it was.

"All will be well." He glanced down at the food in his hands and took a deep whiff. "This looks delicious! Thank you."

She nodded and motioned to the dining table where her soup still sat, cold.

"Won't you join me?" At her hesitation, he pleaded, "Please. I'm sure you need the nourishment. Have you eaten today?"

She hadn't. In fact, she'd forgotten about eating since Mr. Goodman arrived. She shook her head, suddenly feeling very tired.

Mr. Goodman placed his food on the table and pointed to her chair. "Sit down, please. I'll heat up your soup."

She tried to protest but just didn't have the energy. He pulled out the chair for her, and she obliged and sat. Then he removed her bowl, carried it to the kitchen, and returned with it filled with steaming soup. After he placed the bowl in front of her, he seated himself.

He bowed his head and Isabel did likewise.

"Our Father, thank You for this blessing of food, a warm house, and the kindness of this dear lady. Amen."

Isabel nodded. "Amen."

The warm broth trickled down her throat, soothing her. She was glad she'd made it, and happy she had something to offer her guest.

"This is wonderful." Mr. Goodman wasted no time emptying his bowl.

Good as it tasted, Isabel couldn't eat much. She sipped the soup little by little, feeling full despite the small amount.

"So your husband John is the light keeper?" Mr. Goodman asked.

Isabel's spoon fell from her hand, clattering on the table. "The light! I have to light the lantern!"

Isabel stood, but a pain shot through her abdomen, making her breath catch. She grabbed the back of the chair to steady herself. A jolt of fear coursed through her. Was something wrong with the baby?

Mr. Goodman jumped to his feet and rushed to her side. "I don't think you're in any condition to go to the lighthouse."

"But I must! John's not here, and I'll have to do it."

"I'll do it for you. You need to lie down."

Isabel opened her mouth to object but couldn't speak. She leaned against Mr. Goodman for support as he helped her to the parlor, where she lay on the sofa.

"You know what to do?" She gasped for breath.

Mr. Goodman looked down on her, his face glowing with kindness. "I do. I've helped many light keepers before. You just close your eyes and rest. Everything will be fine."

Why did she trust this stranger? Yet she did. His voice conveyed peace. *Fear not* echoed in her mind, so she complied.

* * *

Bright rays of sunlight streaked across the new-fallen snow as John and Mrs. Harris climbed into the boat at dawn and pushed away from town.

"It's a beautiful Christmas morn." John scanned the countryside, cloaked in a blanket of white.

"Yes indeed." Mother Harris nodded. "Snow has a way of making everything look so clean and pure."

"Thank God, we have no wind today, or it'd be much colder." John cut a path through the water with each pull of the oars.

"The sun is warm despite the cold air. We couldn't have asked for a more beautiful day."

Mrs. Harris lifted her face to the sun.

It took little time to cover the distance to the lighthouse on the calm water. John rowed up to the shore, leaped out, and pulled the skiff up on the sand so his mother-in-law could step out on dry land. Her smiled widened as she scanned the surroundings.

"How lovely, John! What a charming little island."

John tied up the boat, then reached for her hand to help her up the slope. "Isabel and I think so, but it's especially pretty today, covered in snow."

"There's smoke coming from the chimney. She must be up and about now," Mother Harris said, looking uphill at the cottage.

"The light is on in the lighthouse." John observed the lantern slowly rotating in the tower nearby. How did she manage to light it? "I better put it out before we go to the house."

* * *

John hurried into the tower and ran up the stairs. He snuffed out the lantern and closed the curtains, then rushed back down where Mother Harris waited at the foot of the stairs.

They continued across the snow to the cottage. When they reached the door, they found it unbolted. John shoved the door open.

"Isabel?" Mother Harris called out as they entered. No one answered. She turned to John, her eyebrows knit together. "Where could she be?"

"Isabel?" John pushed away the encroaching anxiety. What if she had climbed up the stairs and then collapsed with exhaustion?

It took no time for them to realize she wasn't in the parlor or the kitchen. Together they went to the bedroom, John holding his breath. *Please let her be all right.*

Isabel lay still on the bed.

John hurried to her side. "Isabel, are you feeling well?" He clasped her hand, relieved to find it warm.

"Isabel, dear, it's Mother. We're here." She leaned over her daughter's form.

Isabel's eyes fluttered open, then widened.

"Mother?" She turned her head and saw her husband. "John. You're here."

"Yes, we're here, darling." John bent over his wife and kissed her. "I'm sorry we couldn't get here yesterday. The storm proved too rough for us to make the attempt."

A smile eased across Isabel's face as her eyes moistened with tears. "I know, dear. I'm just happy you've arrived safely." Then her smile disappeared. "I'm so sorry about the light, John. I wanted to light it for you, but I was just too tired."

"What do you mean? The light was on when we got here. I just put it out."

Isabel's face brightened. "Mr. Goodman must've done it! He's such a nice man. Have you met him?"

John exchanged glances with Mother Harris, and they both shook their heads.

"We didn't see anyone. Who is Mr. Goodman?" Had a man been in his home with Isabel? John racked his brain trying to remember someone named Goodman.

"He came last night when his boat wrecked on the rocks. He said he knew you from the navy. I was a little scared about letting a stranger in the house at first, but he didn't seem like a stranger. He was more like a friend."

John worked his jaw, certain he didn't know a Goodman. "There's no wrecked boat down below. Where is this Mr. Goodman?"

"I don't know. The last thing I remember is him helping me to the sofa. I wasn't feeling well. He told me not to worry, that he'd light the lantern."

"But where is his boat? How did he leave?" John restrained himself from running out to search for the man.

Isabel moved her head from side to side. "I'm just thankful he was here. He prayed with me, and I felt such peace about your safety and the baby." Her eyes widened. "Oh! I just remembered what he said when he prayed. He asked God to watch over 'John and Mrs. Harris.' Mother, I never told him your name. How did he know?"

"Who is this stranger who claimed to know us?" John asked.

Mother Harris patted Isabel on the hand. "He was an answer to our prayer, John. That's who he was."

Just then, Isabel gasped and cried out, her eyes darting to her mother. "Mother, I think the baby's coming!"

Mother Harris moved closer to her daughter's side and waved John away. "John, you best make yourself scarce for a while. Looks like another prayer is about to be answered, just in time for Christmas."

THE SNOW GLOBE

Ginger Kolbaba

Tina Wayans was tired. She had spent the better part of the morning and afternoon unpacking boxes at the bungalow she and her husband, Mike, had rented on Daisy Street in the small town of Lawrence, Wisconsin. She wasn't sure why she should even bother unpacking. They'd probably be moving again soon enough.

"Hey, babe, I'm home," her husband called from the front door.

"In here."

She could hear Mike trudging through their living room with his boots on.

"Take off your boots, mister. I'm not in the mood to clean up snowy footprints all over the house."

He chuckled, caught. "Sorry."

She heard him pull off each boot and drop it.

He walked into the room, looked around at the boxes still stacked, and gave her a kiss.

"How's it going?"

"The same as every other time." After six moves in three years, Tina was finding it difficult to pretend she enjoyed the task of unpacking and "settling in."

Mike raised an eyebrow.

"Fine, it's great!" Tina said. "I love unpacking. It's my favorite thing in the whole world." She clasped her hands in a mock beg. "Can we please move again soon so I can pack and unpack all over again?"

Mike laughed. "I know. Being married to an army consultant doesn't exactly allow for stability in the home decorating department." He pulled off his jacket to reveal his army fatigues. He looked good. His lean, muscular build and buzz haircut suited her thirty-two-year-old husband.

"Yeah, well, I think I'm going easy on the decorating this time around. That way I'll have less to pack the next time. What, in a month?" Tina didn't mean for it to come out so snarky, but she was worn out and hungry, and that always made her a little cranky.

"Tell you what. Why don't you unpack the Christmas boxes? You could listen to Christmas music—that always puts you in the Christmas spirit. And we can leave the rest of the boxes for later."

Tina shook her head. "It's bad enough constantly doing and undoing our things. Now we add Christmas. I just don't—"

"Come on, babe."

"I'm serious, Mike. What's there to celebrate this year? I don't know anybody here. I'm nowhere close to any of my family or friends—and I won't get to share Christmas with them. For the first time in my twenty-six years, I might add.

I want to settle down. I want to be somewhere long enough where I actually have to dust!"

"Tina." Mike shook his head gently. "You knew this would be our life when you married me."

"I know. And I thought I could handle it. All you need is love and all that. But I also need friends and my family and a little bit of a routine. I can't even get a job since we're never around long enough." She raised her hands in defense. "I know, I know. There's nothing you can do about that, so I should just get over it and finish unpacking."

Mike drew her to him and wrapped his arms around her. "I know this has been difficult for you, and I'm sorry you've had to handle most of it on your own. You're right. For right now, I can't change it. So let's make the best of it, okay?" He kissed the top of her head. "Do the Christmas stuff. Having all the decorations up will make you feel better. It will feel like a home then. I promise."

Tina sighed. She knew he was right. She should at least try to be a little more mature about it all. "Yeah, okay."

"Tell you what, how about I help you decorate? I have a few things going at work, but I can probably squeeze out of them early and we can work on it together. How's that sound?"

She smiled. "Thanks, Mike. That's sweet, but it's okay. I know you've been swamped at work, and hey, what else have I got to do all day? I'll do it. And you're right; I'm sure it will make me feel better."

She doubted it, but at least that's what she hoped.

* * *

Two days later Mike brought home a tree and stored it in the snow in their backyard, "until you're ready for it," he said. But a week passed and Tina still hadn't unpacked the Christmas decorations. Mike would hint about it in the evenings when he got home from work—even re-offering to help her unpack and decorate—but she always declined, and with each hint, she gave an excuse to why she hadn't gotten around to it yet. She had to focus on the window treatments. The laundry needed attention. She had to arrange the spice shelf.

But the truth was that every time she opened a box, sadness swept over her. Christmas without her family. Why remind herself of that with decorations all over the house? What was the point, anyway?

By the end of the week, Tina was making her grocery list for that evening's meal when her cell phone rang.

"Hi, babe." Mike's voice sounded hesitant.

"What's up?"

"I hate to do this to you, but we're working on some time-sensitive items and I don't think I'm going to make it home tonight for supper."

"It's Friday night. We always do dinner and a movie on Fridays."

"I know. And I wouldn't miss it if I had a choice."

"What time do you think you'll be home?"

"I don't know. It could be late."

Tina sighed heavily. "So what am I supposed to do?"

"Well." Mike cleared his throat. "I know you still haven't done anything to make the house Christmassy and—"

"And you want me to put up some decorations, is that it?"

"Well, it would make it nice. Christmas is in a couple of weeks, so it seems appropriate." He paused, then continued quickly, "It doesn't have to be anything spectacular—"

"You got that right."

"Will you at least...try?"

Tina clenched her teeth. "Fine. I'll do my best."

"Thanks, sweetie. This means a lot. I'll make it up to you."

"Yeah, I know. See you tonight." She hit the End key on her phone and leaned hard back in her chair. "Merry Christmas."

She pushed the list away from her on the table, then ran her fingers through her long, thick hair. "Okay, Tina. Guess we can't delay the inevitable anymore, can we?"

She stood slowly and walked to the back bedroom where the Christmas boxes were stored. She would have placed them in the garage or attic or the garbage, but Mike had insisted they sit in the house since Christmas was so close.

She opened the first box and pulled out two bunches of gold and silver garland. Then she grabbed her miniature nut-cracker and soldier set and set them on top of one of the other boxes. She fished through the box, choosing what she'd bring out and what she'd leave behind.

"I may have to decorate, but I'm not going all-out and I'm not going to enjoy it."

She closed that box and moved to the ornaments box. It was filled with green, red, blue, and white shiny bulbs. She pulled those out and then spotted her treasured ornaments—the ones she had collected every year since she was ten. When she was growing up, her parents would buy her an ornament that signified something special that had happened each year. She had an ice skater ornament from when she learned how to skate when she was twelve. The cap and diploma was from the year she graduated from high school. Then she spotted the Precious Moments bride and groom her younger sister gave her three years before when Tina and Mike were married.

The next box held a Nativity set that her grandmother gave her the year before she died. Pulling each piece gingerly from its Styrofoam holder, she placed them on another box, then she sat on the floor. Tears flooded her eyes and threatened to spill onto her cheeks.

"Grandma would skin me alive for not wanting to celebrate the Lord's birthday this year." Slowly she rubbed a hand over her cheek and eye and pulled herself toward the next box.

Glancing at the contents, she didn't spy anything she wanted to use this year, but just as she began to close the box flaps, the glint of something at the bottom caught her eye. She reached in and pulled out a small, ornate snow globe she'd given Mike one year while they were dating. The winter scene depicted a countryside with a cottage nestled in the back and a horse-drawn sleigh, with laughing children running alongside.

Absently, Tina shook the globe and watched the glittery snowflakes dance until they settled on the cottage and horse and ground. She shook it again and watched quietly.

This is my life, she thought. *Shaken and frenzied.*

She knew snow globes offered a serene, peaceful feeling. There seemed to be something hypnotic about shaking them and then watching the snow settle slowly and peacefully all around. But for her, this year it felt more chaotic. Like her life. Just as she'd get used to being in one place, someone somewhere beyond her control would shake the globe and send her world into chaos once again. The snow never seemed to settle but was constantly getting jarred and turned upside down and shaken side to side.

She exhaled, then gathered the decorations in her arms and headed back into the living room. She placed the manger and globe on the mantel and then scattered the other stand-alone decorations around the room. It didn't look overtly Christmassy, but it was something. It would have to do for now, she decided. She'd tackle the tree later.

To clear her head she decided to walk to the town square, about six blocks from her house, to check out a gourmet kitchen shop she'd seen there. She hoped a brisk walk in the winter chill would help her to stop feeling sorry for herself. She grabbed her purse, scarf, and coat and headed out the door.

The sun was just setting as she headed toward the downtown area. The cold air tingled her cheeks. As she passed through her neighborhood, she noticed it seemed every house got into the Christmas spirit. Christmas lights twinkled and outdoor Santas greeted her as she walked by. Several houses had manger scenes or inflatable snowmen. But by the fourth or fifth house she began to see a pattern with one particular type of decoration: large blowup snow globes sat in everyone's front yards. They hummed as they popped snow around the globes like giant popcorn poppers.

She turned a corner and ahead of her she saw a giant lit banner that hung above the street entrance to the town square—Shaken but Never Stirred: Lawrence's Snow Globe Days. Welcome!

She couldn't help but smile. "That explains the snow globes on everyone's lawn," she said aloud. The town square was filled with the same type of large outdoor snow globe decorations. And as she passed each shop, she saw snow globes decorating each window display. Every globe seemed to be unique, each sporting a different and beautiful scene inside. They went from beautiful Thomas Kinkade scenes to outrageous SpongeBob. All sizes and colors and even shapes were represented.

She arrived at Sarah's Gourmet Kitchen shop. Here too were snow globes, all kitchen-related. One was a 1950s kitchen scene with retro appliances. One had a fat French chef holding a loaf of bread and laughing. Another depicted a family of kittens baking cookies.

The shop, though snug and cozy, was packed with every conceivable kitchen utensil. And the smell of coffee and fresh spices filled Tina's nostrils, awakening them with delight as she entered and tried to warm up.

A small bell over the door chimed as she entered, and a plump, red-haired woman in her fifties looked up from price labeling jars of what appeared to be multicolored honey. She put the price label gun on the counter.

"Hello! Welcome to Sarah's Gourmet Kitchen."

"Hi."

"I'm Sarah. Looking for anything in particular today?"

"Just browsing."

"That's good too. We have some great specials going this weekend for the festival. They're all up here." She pointed toward a few baskets to the right of the counter. "Are you in town for the festival?"

Tina shook her head. "My husband and I just moved here a few weeks ago."

Sarah's face lit up. "Well then, a doubly good welcome! And what a great time to move here. We're a small town, but we have a great community, and the Snow Globe Days are the best."

"It's definitely something," Tina said, picking up a penguin-shaped salt shaker paired with a walrus pepper shaker.

"There's just something about snow globes, you know? They just make me smile." Sarah picked up a basket of spiced pretzel samples and offered it to Tina. "Try these."

Tina dipped her hand into the basket, pulled out one of the pretzels, and popped it into her mouth. "Mmm. They *are* good."

"Told you. You definitely want to check out the festivities this evening. They even do a living snow globe. That's mainly for the kids, but everyone loves it. Here, let me grab you a schedule." Sarah darted to the counter and picked up a piece of paper from a short stack by the cash register. "Here you go. And definitely stop by First Community Church tomorrow night for the choir concert and hot cocoa. The church is just a block over. Behind the courthouse. I go there. Since you just moved, you should definitely check us out. You'll need to build up a support system."

Tina couldn't help laughing, or resist as Sarah offered her another pretzel. After Tina dug in, Sarah helped herself to a pretzel as well.

Sarah took a bite, then popped open her eyes wide. "What am I doing? I'm so sorry. I didn't mean to bombard you. Look around! Take your time. I'll be here."

Tina laughed again. "Thanks. And you sold me on those pretzels. I'll take a bag."

Sarah giggled. "I'll put one up for you at the register."

Tina continued to browse the narrow aisles. But as her eyes were taking in all the sights of pots and cake pans and

"Chocolate Rocks!" aprons, her mind was thinking about Sarah's bubbly personality.

I used to feel that way. Happy about everything. She brushed her hand over the yellow-and-green checkered dish towels.

After a few more minutes she chose a small egg-frying pan and miniature spatula and carried them to the front of the store.

"Good choice," Sarah said, ringing her up. "I use my egg pan for making egg sandwiches. They're the perfect size to go on an English muffin."

"I'll have to try that."

Sarah placed everything in a plastic Sarah's Gourmet Kitchen bag. Then she reached across the counter, grabbed a small snow globe that read "Snow Globe Days," and put it in the bag as well.

"Just a little thank-you token. Each shop gives them away during the festival, but some shop owners are a little stingy with theirs and try to sell them to the tourists. I don't think that's right. Anyway, my dear, welcome again to Lawrence. See you at the concert tomorrow night?"

Tina nodded and shrugged. "Maybe. I'll see if my husband has anything planned."

"Well, definitely bring him along! The more the merrier."

They exchanged good-byes, then Tina stepped out of the store and pulled her scarf tighter around her neck. The wind had picked up and flurries filled the air. She saw more people in the square, walking around and looking at the giant snow globes. Johnny Mathis was crooning "Chestnuts roasting on an open fire" through speakers placed strategically throughout the area.

She took a few steps toward home, then stopped. *Why am I rushing home? Mike won't be back until late.* She turned around and began to walk toward the center of the square. She figured she might as well take in the festivities while she was there.

The center of the square was a winter wonderland. Strands of twinkling lights hung from tree limbs and poles, and enormous globes lit the square, humming and bouncing slightly from the wind and the snow bursting around the insides.

Families seemed congregated by a massive square inflatable bounce house that had snow-type balls bounding around. Shrieks of laughter rang out from inside. Tina walked over to catch the action, and after a moment began to watch the parents instead. They all seemed happy, joyous. Without a care in the world.

They probably haven't moved multiple times. They probably get to see their family this Christmas.

The song changed, and she heard Bing Crosby's silky voice. "I'll be home for Christmas…"

You might be, Bing, but I sure won't.

"…if only in my dreams," the song ended.

Suddenly it was all too much. Loneliness and hopelessness washed over her, and Tina gave in to the tears.

I don't want to be here. I don't want this life. I want to go home. I want to have a home, a real home to go to.

She wiped her nose quickly and dropped her head so no one would see her crying, then pushed her way through the crowds toward the house.

* * *

Tina was already in bed by the time Mike came home. She felt him slip in quietly next to her and lean over to kiss her.

"That was a long meeting," she mumbled, half asleep.

"Sorry, I didn't mean to wake you."

"'S okay. Did you get everything handled?"

"Yeah. It took some extra convincing, but I finally got them to see what they needed to do. What'd you do tonight?"

"There's a festival in the square. I walked around there a bit."

"That sounds like fun. Maybe you can show it to me tomorrow?"

"Sure." *Let's add more salt to the wound and remind me of what I don't have.*

* * *

The next day Mike helped her haul the tree in from the backyard and set it up in the front room by the picture window. As he worked out in the garage organizing his space there, Tina slowly, begrudgingly, wrapped the blinking lights around the tree, then took each ornament and placed it on the tree's branches. Then she carefully placed the garland, and finally hooked up the angel and set her at the top.

"Now *that*'s a tree." Mike came up behind her and wrapped his arms around her waist. "Your grandma would be proud."

Tina didn't say anything.

"Babe, I need to run out and do a little shopping. Why don't we plan to go to the festival tonight?"

She nodded. "That's fine." Tears filled her eyes again and she turned away to try to hide them.

"What's wrong?" Mike never missed anything.

"Nothing," she whispered. "I need to get back to unpacking some more of those boxes."

"Forget the boxes. What's going on?"

She snapped. "Seriously, Mike? I'm tired. I'm *exhausted*. I want a home. I want to see my family. I don't want this life anymore!"

"We've already talked about this—"

"I know we have. And I'm telling you, I'm not moving anymore. I walked around that festival last night *by myself*, and all those people, those *families*, were happy. They have lives that aren't constantly being disrupted. They have community. What do I have? A rented house for the next four months. A husband I rarely see. No friends. Just myself. And I'm supposed to be the good wife and just take it. Well, I can't anymore." Tears flowed freely now. "I. Can't."

"What do you want me to do, Tina? Quit my job? Will that make you happy? Do you want to leave and go back to your mom and dad? Will *that* make you happy? What? What do you want me to do? You've been unhappy for most of our marriage now. You've pouted and complained and vented. If I give you what you want, will that do the trick? Somehow I don't think so."

Mike walked over to the hall closet and grabbed his coat. "Maybe the problem isn't me or this marriage or all our moves." He shoved his arms into the coat sleeves. "Maybe the problem is you." He turned and walked out the front door.

Tina stood paralyzed in her place. She wasn't sure what she really wanted, but she wanted to complain. She wanted to feel sorry for herself. She wanted someone to give her sympathy.

She watched him walk down the front path, turn to the left, and disappear.

Glancing around the room at the decorations she'd just put up, she noticed Mike's snow globe. Anger welled up within her, and she grabbed the globe from the mantel and shook it hard. She kept shaking it and shaking it until her arm grew tired, then she slammed it down on the coffee table. It caught the side of a ceramic tree sitting in the center of the table and cracked. The fluid from the inside the globe began to seep out, plastering the snow granules to the bottom and sides.

"Oh no!" Tina rushed to the kitchen to grab a towel. By the time she returned, the liquid had puddled around the coffee table. The globe no longer held the magical joy it once had. Now, it looked dingy, lackluster. Inspecting it, she wondered if there would be any chance to repair it, but she knew it was ruined.

"How's the temper tantrum working for you, Tina?" she asked aloud. This wasn't who she wanted to be. This wasn't who she *was,* but somehow she'd allowed herself to become that person she didn't like. She'd always been easygoing, flexible. Now she felt like that broken globe. Drained.

She carried the globe to the kitchen and set it on the counter.

Well, I know what I should get Mike for Christmas. And she knew exactly where to get another one.

She grabbed her snow boots and coat and scarf and wrapped herself up, then took her purse and headed back to the festival. Surely they'd have snow globes for sale.

She walked back toward the square. As she drew closer, she could hear the Christmas music and humming globes grow louder and more joyous. Not sure where to start, she decided to go back to Sarah's Gourmet Kitchen to see if the bubbly woman had any suggestions for the best place to buy snow globes.

The bell above the door chimed and Sarah called out from the back of the shop, "Hello! Welcome to Sarah's Gourmet Kitchen. I'll be with you in a moment!" Tina could hear her chatting with another customer, so she walked to the counter and stood.

Within a minute Sarah scurried up the far aisle. "Coming!" As soon as she spotted Tina, she let out a big laugh. "Well, hello, stranger! Back for more pretzels?" She was wearing dangling miniature snow globe earrings, a headband that had reindeer antlers, and an apron that said Santa's List: Naughty or Nice?

"Nice apron." Tina couldn't seem to take her eyes off Sarah's earrings. Sarah noticed Tina's gaze and instinctively brought her hand to her left ear. "Like these? It took me forever to find them. Look, every time I shake my head, the snow goes crazy. Fun, huh?"

"Yeah, definitely catchy."

"Did you enjoy the festival last night?"

"I did. Thanks. Hey, I was wondering if you knew where I could pick up a snow globe."

Sarah burst out laughing. "That's the best question I've had all day!"

Tina chuckled a little. "I mean, which store will have the best selection? I figured I'd ask you rather than go from shop to shop."

"Oh! That makes more sense. You really had me, though." She laughed again. "I'd say Gilmer's Crafters. Turn right, go half a block. You can't miss it."

"Thanks." Tina turned to leave.

"Hold on a sec." Sarah disappeared down an aisle, then returned with a bag of yogurt-covered pretzels. "Here, take these. You'll love them. They have a secret ingredient in the yogurt." Her eyes glanced heavenward. "Addictive."

"I can't take these."

"Sure you can. Don't tell anyone, though. It's a Christmas present." Sarah studied her. "You look like you could use one. And maybe a friend too?"

Stunned, Tina stared at the store owner.

Sarah smiled knowingly and patted Tina's arm. "Honey, I don't know what you're going through, but I can tell it's something. The gals at church say I have a gift that way—reading people. It doesn't take much reading to know that you just moved, you have to unpack, and you're probably stressed out of your mind. Am I right?"

Tina's eyes widened. She opened her mouth to say something, but then closed it again and merely nodded.

"I thought so," Sarah went on. "Are you going to the concert tonight?" Before Tina could respond, Sarah continued. "Go. It will do you good. I promise. I'll be there. Save you a seat?"

Tina nodded again.

"Good girl. Tell Marsha over at Gilmer's I said hi. She'll help you."

Tina turned and held up the pretzels. Before she could say thanks, Sarah said, "You're welcome. Merry Christmas."

Gilmer's Crafters was exactly where Sarah said it would be. Its shelves in the display windows were overflowing with snow globes and brightly wrapped Christmas presents. She entered the store and saw that an entire aisle was designed for the globes. They had premade and do-it-yourself globes, along with Christmas jewelry, T-shirts, candy, and tacky Christmas knickknacks. She hoped against hope that somehow, miraculously, they'd have an exact replica of the globe she'd broken. They had similar scenes but nothing exactly the same. She picked out one with a horse-drawn sleigh and cottage, but no laughing children, and took it to the counter to purchase it. Then she glanced at her watch. The concert would be starting in a half hour.

She thought about going home. Mike might have returned and would wonder where she was. But his words still stung. Instead she pulled her cell phone out of her purse and called him. When he didn't pick up, she left a message telling him where she'd gone and that he was welcome to join her if he wanted.

* * *

The church was an old building with a tall steeple and stained-glass windows. The doors to the sanctuary were open and the waiting crowd began to herd in. A balding man handed Tina a program, and she found a seat toward the back and settled in.

To pass the time Tina perused the program. It was filled with advertising from the town's shops, a note from the mayor about the festival, and an invitation to attend the church that Sunday.

"There you are!" Sarah squeezed in past Tina to take a seat. "I was supposed to save you a seat, but it looks like you beat me to it. No husband tonight?"

Tina shook her head. "I don't think so. I left him a voice mail, but he hasn't gotten back to me."

"Well, we can hold a spot for him."

A door to the side of the stage opened and men and women in red choir robes filed into the room, carrying black folders, and took their place on risers at the center of the stage.

A middle-aged man in a tuxedo and bright-red bow tie walked through the door, and the crowd began to applaud. He smiled broadly and bowed, then turned very serious and faced the choir. As his hands raised, the choir opened their folders and looked expectantly at him.

A teenager from the front row walked to the Christmas tree at the side of the stage and plugged it in. A thousand tiny bulbs lit the tree in an explosion of color, and suddenly the choir, singing as one voice, burst into song: "Sing we now of Christmas."

The hair on Tina's arms stood up. The sound was so simple, but so sacred and beautiful. For the next hour she was enthralled by the music and stories. The folks in the small town weren't professional by any stretch, but they were passionate and loved this tradition. Finally, the pastor stood and walked to the front of the stage.

"Many people dread this time of year," he said. "They've lost loved ones, or the pressures of the season and the expectations weigh down upon them. People put pressure on themselves to be or do something they really don't want. But if the real Christmas meaning is anything, it's about authenticity. It's when we strip away all the facade, all the pretense, and we kneel in front of a humble, unimpressive manger to worship a king who was everything and became nothing. For us."

The pastor walked over to a table at the side of the stage and picked up a snow globe. He shook it gently and held it up.

"This weekend our town celebrates Snow Globe Days. We love looking at these things, don't we? There's something hypnotic about them. When my daughter was three, she was completely enamored with snow globes. She would shake them and let them settle, and then shake them again. Over and over she did that. It wouldn't have been so bad, but this particular snow globe also played music when you shook it. For hours all my wife and I would hear was, 'Let it snow, let it snow, let it snow' in voices that sounded like the munchkins from *The Wizard of Oz*."

The audience laughed.

"While snow globes are fun to play with and watch, they also seem to speak to many people's lives. We see the serene scenes in the globe and the lovely snow that falls all around, but in order to get the snow to fall, we have to do what? Shake things up, don't we?"

Tina sat up a little straighter in her seat. The pastor seemed to be speaking directly to her.

"Snow globes are wonderful reminders that in the midst of the chaos of life, there's intense beauty. But here's the important lesson. Often we can't really ever appreciate the beauty until we go through the chaos. We can't watch the snow fall in the snow globe unless and until we shake the globe. We can't appreciate the goodness of our lives unless and until we accept that in our lives we must experience a little shaking up."

The pastor walked to the other side of the stage, where a manger scene was displayed.

"How are you handling the chaos and shaking up in your life?"

Not too well, Tina thought, looking down at the program she'd rolled tightly in her hands.

The pastor motioned to the back. "Service hosts, would you begin?" He smiled and looked back at the audience. "We have a gift for you. This is to remember that when the chaos and the shaking come, you have something to lean on."

Several people started to walk down the aisles, each carrying a large velvet bag. As one of the hosts got to Tina's row, he dipped into the bag and pulled out enough snow globes for each person in her row. She passed them down and then took hers. The globe had a manger with a star hanging over it. The star was in the shape of a cross. And across the top of the globe it said, "Love reigns."

The choir started to hum "Silent Night" as the pastor continued. "Whatever you're going through," he said, "love reigns. You know, for many people Christmas can be the loneliest time of the year. If you're feeling lonely, or overwhelmed, or whatever you're experiencing, I want you to hold up this snow globe and remember that God loves you and goes with you through all the chaos. And with that kind of love, you will never truly be alone."

With those words, the pastor turned to the choir and nodded. The choir sang the words to the venerable carol. "Silent night, holy night. All is calm, all is bright..."

Tina sat stunned. She looked at the globe in her hands. *Love reigns.*

Maybe Mike was right. She'd spent so much time pitying herself and focused on the negative that she failed to see the good things. Maybe all the cross-country moves and packing and unpacking really did have a positive side. They'd taught her to hold loosely to things. She got to experience life and people in different parts of the country—something many people never had the opportunity to experience. Despite her complaints, she *had* made friends with every move.

All of a sudden, Tina wanted to go home. She put the globe and program in her purse and started to get up.

"Where're you going?" Sarah whispered.

"Home," Tina said, smiling as she said the word. Suddenly it had new meaning.

"But you'll miss the best part! The choir is going to sing the 'Hallelujah Chorus.' And the cocoa. You can't miss that!"

"I've already seen the best part. Now I need to make some things right with my husband."

Sarah smiled and nodded her understanding.

"Plus, I know where to get some of that cocoa anyway." Tina winked.

Tina walked briskly out of the church. She wanted to get home as soon as she could. She was bursting inside with wanting to tell Mike that he was right. That she was sorry. That she'd messed up her priorities. She wanted to tell him so many things. She began to run.

* * *

The house was dark when Tina arrived at her front door. A knot of disappointment settled in her stomach when she realized Mike still wasn't home. She fiddled for her key and dejectedly opened the door.

As she walked into the living room, she saw something move at the couch. She jumped and screamed.

"Whoa, it's me!" Mike's voice came quickly.

"What are you doing in the dark?" She could see his silhouette stand and face her.

"I needed to think."

"In the dark?"

He shrugged. "I need to apologize."

"No, you don't. Me first."

"No, Tina. Let me say this and just hear me out. I can't change my job or that we move all the time. Those things are out of my control. But what has been in my control, I've let slide—and that's my sympathy. As an army brat and then in the army myself, my whole life has been moving and settling and resettling. I'm used to it, and I've never taken the time to really understand how difficult it's been for you. I have the army. But you've had no one."

She was silent, waiting for him to continue. When he didn't, she asked, "Can I turn on a light?"

He laughed and turned on a lamp on their end table.

"Thank you for saying that. That really does mean a lot, Mike. But now I need to say something too." She could see his shoulders tense up, so she rushed ahead. "What you said earlier is true. My attitude has been the problem. I haven't made our marriage easier. And I really do love our marriage. And you. I've made my self-pity my best friend. And I haven't given our"—she held up her fingers in quote marks—"'adventures' a chance. I'm sorry."

He hugged her tightly. "I got you something." He ran into the bedroom and came out with a bag that said Gilmer's Crafters.

A puzzled look crossed her face as she took the bag from him.

"I was going to give it to you for Christmas." He seemed apologetic. "It's nothing, really...I just thought...After I left the house I walked down to the festival. I saw this and...I don't know."

In the bag was a small snow globe. Inside the globe was a couple holding hands and smiling. At the couple's feet was one word spelled in fancy cursive: *Love*.

Tina's laughter filled the house as she grabbed her Gilmer's Crafters bag and then riffled through her purse to pull out the Love Reigns globe.

"Here," she handed him the two globes.

He looked at them and then laughed too. "I guess we should—"

"Start a collection!" they both said.

"If we never move again"—Tina raised her eyebrows and smiled—"or, okay, if we continue to move every six months, you and I have each other. I married you to be with you."

Mike kissed her gently on the lips. He leaned back to take in her face, as if he were trying to decide something. Then he nodded slightly. "I had another surprise for you." He paused again and then grinned. "I worked it out for your family to be here for Christmas."

Tina blinked, as if not understanding. "My family is... wait, what? Really?" Tears welled even as her face broke out in a huge smile.

Mike nodded. "I've been working on it for about a month. They're coming Christmas Eve."

Tina screamed and started to jump up and down. "I can't believe it! You're amazing." She threw her arms around him and squeezed hard. "I'm so lucky to have you."

Cat stepped up behind her. "Maybe *J* has had enough of resort-hopping and decided to come home."

She thought for a moment. After all the scuttlebutt, surely someone would have alerted her that one very tan gentleman wearing Bermuda shorts and a Hawaiian shirt had arrived in town. She laughed, thinking about Jimmy Popchek and his in-depth article.

"What's so funny?" Cat asked.

"Oh, nothing. Just thinking about the characters in this town."

"Enough said."

The sound of crackling brush startled them both.

"It's a right beautiful scene, even if I do say so myself."

Olivia turned. "Are you responsible for this beautiful display, Henry?"

He rocked on his heels, his pride evident. "Ran an extension cord over to my garage." He pointed to the long orange cord running through the snow between the houses. "I figure if her son comes home, he's going to be shocked to find his mother gone. Thought maybe this'd soften the blow."

All three turned their gazes back to the simple white house with its Christmas lights twinkling in the twilight. A large decal of the baby in a manger had been affixed to the front picture window, and even the front door wore a big red bow. "You're a good man, Henry," Olivia said, patting him on the shoulder.

"Wait." He pulled a crumpled piece of paper out of his pocket. "This is for you."

Olivia crinkled her brow and accepted the paper. "What is it?"

"That's why I kept pushing you to decorate."

"Oh! Now it makes sense."

"Just make sure you act surprised when your mom and dad show up at the door, okay?"

She crossed her heart and lifted her hand. "I promise."

She laughed again, then glanced back at the snow globe. Her smile turned into a satisfied grin.

"You know, I learned something tonight from a snow globe."

"Really?"

Tina picked up the Love Reigns globe and cradled it. "We have so much to celebrate in this life—that's true even if we *were* going to spend Christmas without my family. And sometimes we can't really appreciate it until we view it through the midst of upheaval."

"That's some snow globe lesson."

"You bet."

They looked at each for a long moment.

"Wait, don't you owe me a date to the festival?" Tina asked.

"Weren't you just there?"

She smiled. "Yes. But there's a great secret cocoa recipe we need to try. And I know just the place."

She grabbed both their coats and started for the door, then stopped.

"Hold on," she said, turning back into the room. She ran to the tree and plugged in the lights. Then she took the three globes and placed them on the mantel, shaking each one before setting them down.

"Now I'm ready." Tina held out her hand and led Mike out the front door and into their evening's small-town adventure.

About the Authors

Julie Carobini ("Postcards at Christmas") has written five novels set by the sea. *Romantic Times Book Reviews* says, "Carobini has a talent for creating characters that come alive." Married to Dan and mom to three, she loves all things coastal (except sharks). Visit her at juliecarobini.com or facebook.com/authorjuliecarobini.

Linda S. Clare ("The Best Dead Christmas Tree") is the author of women's fiction, including *The Fence My Father Built* and *A Sky Without Stars*. She teaches writing and lives in the Northwest with her family and three wayward cats. Visit her at lindasclare.com, at facebook.com/Lindaclarebooks, or @Lindasclare on Twitter.

Ashley Clark ("The Christmas Thief") writes stories with Southern grace. When she's not writing, Ashley enjoys teaching literature courses at her local university, rescuing stray animals, and finding charming new towns. She lives in Florida with her husband and two rescued dogs, Maddie and Schroeder. Learn more about Ashley at ashleyclarkfiction.com.

JOHNNIE ALEXANDER DONLEY ("Beneath the Christmas Star") is the author of *Where Treasure Hides*. Her writing awards include the prestigious ACFW Genesis Contest (Historical Category, 2011). A longtime Florida resident, she enjoys family get-togethers, classic movies, road trips, and stacks of books. Visit her blog at johnniedonley.com.

PAM HANSON & BARBARA ANDREWS ("Calling Grandma Jean") are a daughter-mother team who have been writing together for many years. They have written more than forty books, including volumes in Guideposts' Tales from Grace Chapel Inn and Miracles of Marble Cove series.

LIZ JOHNSON ("Meat Loaf and Other Minor Miracles") is the author of five novels and a handful of short stories. An Arizona native, she moved to Nashville, Tennessee, three years ago and enjoys exploring the Southern hospitality, harmonies, and history that Music City offers at Christmas and all year long.

GINGER KOLBABA ("The Snow Globe") has written, collaborated, or contributed to more than twenty books, including *Desperate Pastors' Wives*, *A Matter of Wife and Death*, and *Katt's in the Cradle*. Former award-winning editor of *Today's Christian Woman* and *Marriage Partnership*, she now writes and speaks full-time. Visit her at gingerkolbaba.com.

MARILYN TURK ("A Stranger's Visit to the Lighthouse") has been published in *Guideposts* magazine, *A Joyful Heart* (a Guideposts devotional), *The Upper Room*, *Clubhouse Jr.*, and several *Chicken Soup for the Soul* books, and has written two novels. Fascinated by lighthouses, she created a weekly lighthouse blog at marilynturk.com. She lives in Florida with her husband, Chuck, and enjoys fishing and tennis when she's not climbing lighthouses.

A Note from the Editors

We hope you enjoy *A Cup of Christmas Cheer*, created by the Books and Inspirational Media Division of Guideposts, a nonprofit organization that touches millions of lives every day through products and services that inspire, encourage, help you grow in your faith, and celebrate God's love in every aspect of your daily life.

Thank you for making a difference with your purchase of this book, which helps fund our many outreach programs to military personnel, prisons, hospitals, nursing homes, and educational institutions. To learn more, visit GuidepostsFoundation.org.

We also maintain many useful and uplifting online resources. Visit Guideposts.org to read true stories of hope and inspiration, access OurPrayer network, sign up for free newsletters, download free e-books, join our Facebook community, and follow our stimulating blogs.

To learn about other Guideposts publications, including the best-selling devotional *Daily Guideposts*, go to ShopGuideposts.org, call (800) 932-2145, or write to Guideposts, PO Box 5815, Harlan, Iowa 51593.